Tainted
Love

By Melody Mayer

The Nannies
Friends with Benefits
Have to Have It
Tainted Love

Tainted Love

by Melody Mayer

Delacorte Press

Published by Delacorte Press
an imprint of Random House Children's Books
a division of Random House, Inc.
New York

This is a work of fiction. Names, characters, places, and incidents either are the product of the author's imagination or are used fictitiously. Any resemblance to actual persons, living or dead, events, or locales is entirely coincidental.

The author of the balloonist's prayer is unknown. According to www.ballooning.org, it is believed to be adapted from an old Irish sailors' prayer.

Delacorte Press and colophon are registered trademarks of Random House, Inc.

www.randomhouse.com/teens
Educators and librarians, for a variety of teaching tools, visit us at
www.randomhouse.com/teachers

Library of Congress Cataloging-in-Publication Data

Mayer, Melody.
Tainted love : a nannies novel / Melody Mayer. — 1st ed.
p. cm.
Summary: Three seventeen-year-old nannies to the rich and famous
in Beverly Hills wrestle with moral dilemmas over boyfriends, competition,
and telling the truth.
ISBN-13: 978-0-385-73352-6 (trade pbk.)
ISBN-13: 978-0-385-90367-7 (glb edition)
[1. Nannies—Fiction. 2. Interpersonal relations—Fiction. 3. Wealth—Fiction.
4. Beverly Hills (Calif.)—Fiction. I. Title.
PZ7.M4619Tai 2007
[Fic]—dc22
2006023724

The text of this book is set in 11.25-point Berkeley Oldstyle.
Printed in the United States of America
10 9 8 7 6 5 4 3 2 1
First Edition

For my great-grandfather's young writers,
who made him happy
only with the sound of their typewriters clicking

Tainted Love

Kiley McCann

"I should have told you before—I don't actually know how to salsa," Kiley McCann blurted out as Jorge Valdez put his hand on the small of her back to guide her through the thick crowd near the front door of the Conga Room, a salsa dance club on Wilshire Boulevard. Her friend Esme Castaneda was in front of them both, leading the way with her boyfriend, Jonathan Goldhagen.

Jorge just smiled, but Esme looked over her shoulder and gave Kiley an arch look. "Salsa's not so big in Wisconsin, eh?"

"Only on taco chips washed down with a six-pack," Kiley joked. After all, Esme already knew that Kiley's hometown of La Crosse, Wisconsin, was famous for its beer and that her father in fact worked at the local brewery—that is, when he was sober enough to work at all.

Kiley had made two close girlfriends since she'd arrived in Los Angeles two months before. One was Esme, a beautiful and extraordinarily self-sufficient Latina girl who'd grown up in the tough Echo Park section of East Los Angeles. If your car stopped running, or you broke a stiletto heel and needed an emergency repair, Esme always seemed to know just how to fix it. The other was Lydia Chandler—smart, bold, blond, and striking. Born rich, Lydia had been raised in the Amazon rain forest after her parents moved to Amazonia to be medical missionaries. All three girls were nannies to wealthy Los Angeles families. They'd met at the Brentwood Hills Country Club and had become fast friends.

"Check out the drum." Jorge indicated a fifteen-foot-tall conga drum that hung over the entrance like a giant talisman of good times to come. Meanwhile, Santana's "Corazón Espinado" poured through the exterior speakers, mixing with the sounds of the nighttime traffic on Wilshire.

"I love this song!" Esme exclaimed. Eyes narrowed, she swayed to the music, hands overhead, as she moved forward with the crowd. Kiley saw Jonathan give Esme an appreciative look.

Let's face it, Kiley thought. *She's curvy and sultry and hot. Unlike, say, me.*

As Jorge and Jonathan talked to the bulky, bald Latino doorman—Jorge said he was able to get them on the guest list because his public defender father had once defended the owner's best friend on drug charges—Kiley took in the sexy outfits of those in line. Jorge had informed her that the dress code for this club was upscale casual. Kiley had no idea what that meant, so she'd called Esme for details. "Tight skirts, spike heels, shirt unbuttoned down to there, that sort of thing," Esme had filled in.

That was no help. Kiley didn't own a skirt or heels. It felt like playing dress-up when she wore a shirt unbuttoned down to *there*. Finally, she'd made the selection from the meager wardrobe she'd brought with her—one that had been barely supplemented by the occasional shopping expedition with her friends.

Esme and Lydia tried to help her upgrade her wardrobe, but Kiley was saving every penny toward her goal. She'd come to California to qualify for in-state tuition at the famed Scripps Institution of Oceanography. She had one more year of high school, as did her two friends. If she saved diligently, maybe she could graduate from Scripps without a sinkhole of debt.

So, what to wear. She owned exactly two "sexy" items of clothing, both of which had been acquired here in Los Angeles. One was the bottle-green velvet camisole that the producers of the *Platinum Nanny* reality TV show had purchased for her. The other was a plunging white silk shirt that her rock star boss, Platinum, had literally taken off her own back and bestowed on Kiley before a date.

Kiley opted for the white shirt and added one of her three pairs of no-name jeans, then considered her two choices of footwear—Doc Martens or Converse All Stars. Both looked incredibly stupid. Then forces greater than her intervened. That is, she dropped a silver earring, which skidded across the polished wooden floor of her guesthouse bedroom at Platinum's estate and wound up so far under the mahogany dresser that she had to move the furniture to retrieve it. Back against the wall, she found not just her earring but a pair of silver sandals with kitten heels that probably had belonged to some long-dismissed former nanny. Platinum fired employees the way other people changed their thongs.

Miraculously, the sandals were nearly the right size, though the sling-backs pinched her heels something fierce. She was definitely not a suffer-for-beauty kind of girl, but she wore them. She had to.

Even with the sexy shirt and too-small heels, Kiley felt she paled—pun intended—in comparison to Esme. Her friend had twisted her long dark waves up onto her head and stabbed them with a rhinestone barrette; sexy tendrils fell down her back and around her golden face. She wore a red halter shirt that ended just below her bust and a black pencil skirt that fell to just below her knees, slit up the back so that her perfect legs showed when she walked. In very high black heels, she seemed utterly confident.

Kiley knew that wasn't true, of course. Esme had insecurities like everyone else; she just hid hers better than most people. For example, Esme wasn't all that confident about her relationship with Jonathan Goldhagen, who happened to be her very rich employers' son.

Their tickets secured, the velvet rope was moved aside. Jorge took Kiley's hand and led her into the club. "Did I tell you how nice you look?"

She nodded, smiling. When he'd picked her up at Platinum's in his bomber of an old Chevy, he had complimented her immediately. "Nice" was such a bland word, though. "Fantastic" would have been good. Or "hot." "Hot" would have been excellent. Not that Kiley would have believed him. But still.

"Don't sweat the salsa thing," Jorge assured her. "They give lessons. Or I can teach you. It isn't hard."

For you, maybe, Kiley thought as they made their way into the front bar called Caliente Island, the first of many rooms that comprised the club. The walls were chili-pepper red, the cocktail tables round discs of dark wood that sat atop large drums. It was packed with even more of the young, beautiful, blond, and thin, as opposed to how Kiley saw herself: brownish reddish hair, brown eyes, slightly-below-average height, more than slightly pear-shaped, and utterly unsophisticated. By La Crosse standards, she'd been a seven, maybe. By Hollywood standards, she figured she was more like a four point nine.

"Straight through that door." Jorge pointed to an archway that led into the main ballroom. There was a large stage at the far end of the room. Tables banking the dance floor were set on raised platforms behind iron railings. Music that Kiley didn't recognize wailed through the sound system as she saw a small group on the dance floor, gathered around a handsome Latin couple dressed in black and silver lamé. The couple was teaching the group basic—very basic—salsa steps.

"Lessons or tapas before the show?" Jorge asked as they found their reserved black roundtop and sat down.

"Tapas are—" Esme began.

"Little appetizers," Kiley filled in, glad she wasn't totally ignorant. She eyed the female dance teacher, whose round hips swiveled seductively to the music, and doubted very much that she could copy that motion either vertically in public or horizontally in the dark. Not that she knew yet exactly how she'd act horizontally in the dark, but she had a vivid imagination. Even if she could picture it, shouldn't she be picturing it with Tom Chappelle, who was supposed to be her boyfriend (even though he'd been off on a slew of East Coast modeling assignments for the last several weeks), rather than with Jorge Valdez, who was supposed to be just a friend?

"Tapas," Kiley decided.

"Me too. I'll take this one," Jonathan declared as he looped an arm around Esme and kissed her cheek. He was tall and rangy, with the broad shoulders and easy gait of a natural athlete. His perfect golden tan, acquired from hours on the tennis court or aboard his parents' yacht, highlighted his startlingly pale blue eyes. He wore a baby blue linen shirt with the sleeves rolled up, and faded Ralph Lauren jeans. "Something tells me she doesn't need salsa lessons."

"Está en mi sangre," Esme replied, giving Jonathan a soft kiss.

"It's in my . . . something," Jonathan translated.

"Blood," Jorge filled in.

Jonathan shrugged. "What can I tell you? I got a C in high school Spanish. Even that was a gift."

"Fortunately you have other redeeming qualities," Esme informed him, and they kissed again.

Kiley looked away. She was happy that Esme and Jonathan were now officially a couple—and had been for the better part of six weeks—but any and all PDAs made her uncomfortable, especially when she was on a date with Jorge.

The raven-haired waitress came by to take their drink orders—Kiley asked for a virgin Long Island iced tea and thought about how she'd introduced the drink to her mom when she'd been in Los Angeles. Kiley's mom was a waitress at a truck-stop diner just outside La Crosse called the Derby and suffered from a serious anxiety disorder. Often, her panic attacks kept her from doing the simplest things, like shopping at the mall or going to the movies.

But I still owe her, big-time.

Even with the panic attacks, Jeanne McCann had accompanied Kiley to Los Angeles so that she could be on the reality TV show designed to choose a new nanny for über–rock legend Platinum. Through each elimination round, she'd stood by her daughter's side, even when the producers did their best to make Kiley look stupid for the cameras. When the show got canceled before it ever got on the air—something about focus groups giving it a big thumbs-down—she'd been right there to comfort her daughter. Most of all, when the champagne-guzzling, notoriously bed-hopping star offered Kiley the job anyway, Jeanne McCann had actually said yes. Even after that, when disaster struck, she hadn't ordered Kiley home.

"So, what do you think?" Jorge asked, pulling Kiley out of her reverie. Eighteen, with smooth skin the color of rich caramel, Jorge had deep-set eyes that seemed to look inside whomever he was talking to. He was going into his senior year at Esme's old school in Echo Park. "Of the club?"

"It's pretty cool. So . . . how's your aunt doing?" she asked, waiting for the drinks and tapas to come.

"Eighty years old and still works for *La Raza* every day." He chuckled ruefully. "When I'm eighty, I want to be on the south coast of Spain, telling stories about my wild youth. You getting along any better with the colonel?"

Kiley groaned. The colonel was Platinum's brother-in-law.

After Platinum had been arrested for having drugs in her home, the colonel and his wife, Susan—Platinum's sister—had come to Los Angeles to save the three kids from even temporary foster care. He ran the household like marine boot camp. It was everything Kiley could do to keep the kids from executing a coup d'état with live ammunition.

"I say 'yes, sir' and 'no, sir' a lot; try to stay on schedule and out of his way," Kiley replied, shaking her head. "The man probably showers in full combat gear."

Jorge chuckled. "Doesn't exactly make you want to enlist, eh?"

"Do they even have marine biologists in the military?"

She considered that for a moment. She was definitely going to become a marine biologist, or choose another career that satisfied her great love for the ocean. She hadn't really considered it before, but the military would be one way to reach her goal. She had a cousin who'd joined the National Guard to help pay for college. Of course, he got sent to the Persian Gulf, and was still there.

"I don't think I'm military material."

"I know, I know, you're going to Scripps," Esme singsonged.

Kiley nodded emphatically. "Somehow, some way."

"I like that about you," Jorge acknowledged. "Determination. It gets you places." He stood and held out his hand. "Dance?"

Kiley glanced at the dance floor, where a handful of couples were swaying to a low, seductive song. *What the hell.*

"Sure."

When one arm slid around her and the other took her hand, it was the first time Jorge had done more than touch her lightly or offer a fraternal hug. To Kiley's surprise, his arms felt wonderful. He was only a couple inches taller than her, and he smelled clean, like soap. He wasn't tall and broad like Tom. Yet they fit just fine.

"So, the Latin Kings are doing a gig next weekend," he said after they'd swayed together for a while. He was talking about his rap group. "That's the date we missed when I went to Texas. I thought you might want to come."

"Let me check with the colonel. Call me."

"Excellent." He hummed as they danced. "I was wondering. How is it that you fell so in love with the ocean?"

"The one and only family trip we ever took," Kiley explained. "To San Diego. I saw the ocean for the first time and . . . something just clicked for me. I can't explain it."

"Maybe you were a mermaid in a former life," Jorge teased.

"Maybe I was on the *Titanic*," she shot back.

"Interesting. Tell me, if you were Rose, would you have fallen in love with poor-but-proud Jack?"

"Of course," Kiley replied. "That is, after I got my degree and an excellent job so I wasn't dependent on poor-but-proud Jack."

Jorge threw his head back and laughed. "Very practical. I thought all girls were romantic."

Kiley knew herself to be ridiculously romantic, though it wasn't a quality she emphasized. If she wasn't so romantic, would she have fallen so hard for Tom, or been so hurt when he couldn't seem to decide just how serious he was about her? No. She would have simply jumped his bones and enjoyed it, no strings. That was certainly what Lydia would do. But though she was in Jorge's arms, she still thought about Tom.

He was probably right that second at a South Beach nightclub with some of the most beautiful girls in the world, partying after a photo shoot, probably—

"Kiley? Where did you go?" Jorge prompted.

"What?"

"You looked a million miles away."

Yeah. South Florida. With a hot male model.

Not that she'd say that aloud. Or even admit the thought. In fact, she was about to suggest they go back to Esme and Jonathan when she found her mouth very occupied. Jorge was kissing it. She was startled. But just when she began to think that it was weird, that she really should explain about Tom, Kiley found herself kissing Jorge back.

2

Esme Castaneda

Twenty-two hours later, Esme and Jonathan were walking hand in hand along the Santa Monica Third Street Promenade. Teeming with shoppers, tourists, and street performers out to earn donated dollars from passersby, the promenade was one of the few places in all of Los Angeles where folks on a stroll didn't have to worry about a stray BMW or Jaguar mowing them down because the driver was busy repairing her MAC lip gloss or overly involved in a cell phone conversation.

Though the sun had set a half hour before, the evening was still warm; hot Santa Ana winds had been blowing from the east for the past two days. The Forest Service had closed all the wilderness areas outside the city to camping and vehicles, fearing that even a stray spark could touch off a brush fire that could spread quickly into a conflagration.

Here in Santa Monica, though, the night was idyllic. Esme and Jonathan had just eaten dinner at the famous Broadway Deli, sharing a pastrami sandwich and a plate of kasha varnishkes topped with the most delicious brown gravy she'd ever tasted. Dessert had been cheesecake with fresh strawberries.

She wasn't thinking about the six-year-old Goldhagen twins, Easton and Weston, adopted in June from Colombia. Diane Goldhagen and her TV producer husband Steven had taken them to their aunt's place in Pacific Palisades for a sleep-over. It meant that Esme had a rare night to herself. Her only orders were to pick the girls up in the morning, since Steven would be limoed to the set of one of his shows and Diane had an appointment at nine in Manhattan Beach.

"Great night, huh?" Jonathan asked. He stopped so that they could join a ragged circle of people around a chubby blues guitarist wearing dirty jeans and a faded Neville Brothers T-shirt. "I've seen this guy before. Check it out—his right hand."

Esme peered at the portly and somewhat unkempt musician. He was perched on a battered black plastic milk crate, cradled an old electric guitar hooked up to a portable amp, and held a guitar pick between two fingers. No. They weren't fingers. The guitarist had stubs where fingers should have been.

"Birth defect," Jonathan explained. "I've talked to him. He calls himself Ti-Ti Fingers. He's fantastic."

Esme watched, fascinated, as Ti-Ti started to play. His stubs flew over the strings, the pick ringing out clear notes while the fingers of his normal left hand danced on the frets. She couldn't imagine going through life that way. Then she thought of all the people she knew back in Echo Park who had been disfigured by industrial accidents, military service, car crashes, or just because they'd been on the wrong side of a turf war. The guy who lived three bungalows away had lost both his legs in Iraq. Over on Jorge's block, a guy who'd been in her class sophomore year had been shot in a drive-by and had a pair of scarred sockets where his eyes used to be. Yet he eschewed sunglasses, treating his wounds as twin badges of honor.

"You know anyone who went to Iraq?" Esme asked Jonathan. "Or who's there now?"

"No. Can't say I do."

"I know lots. Joaquin Marcos. Estrella Gonzalves. Paco Guerra. They're all over there now. Correction. Paco's in Afghanistan."

He looked puzzled. "Strange subject for a nice night. What's that about?"

She shrugged. "Just thinking about different worlds. Yours. And mine."

"Hey, you live on my parents' estate now," Jonathan pointed out. "Not in the barrio."

Esme prickled, even though she knew Jonathan hadn't meant to be the least bit offensive. It was true—she had her own guesthouse on the enormous Goldhagen estate high in the hills of Bel Air. But she felt guilty from time to time, too. It was as if she was abandoning her real people, her real life. She missed being surrounded by Spanish-speaking people; all the sights and smells and tastes of her own culture. Working for the Goldhagens, caring for the twins, and living in Bel Air was the opportunity of a lifetime. In the fall, she'd be attending Bel Air High School, one of the best public schools in Southern California.

Esme knew all the pros of her situation. Her old life—her former gangbanger boyfriend, her business of creating tattoos for members of Los Locos while not working up to her full potential at Echo Park High School—seemed more like a lifetime ago than the two and a half months it had been.

Still, Jonathan wasn't exactly telling it like it was. In her new life, she was the hired help who had come perilously close to being fired on more than one occasion. She worked for the same people as her Mexican parents, who weren't even in America on valid visas. Esme cared for the kids, her mother cooked the food, her father landscaped and fixed things that needed fixing. The entire Castaneda family was dependent on the goodwill of the Goldhagens.

No. Jonathan hadn't told it like it was. That dependency—something he'd never felt in his whole overprivileged life—was the part of the equation that Esme hated most. To make matters worse, she had fallen head over heels for him. He was twenty, an up-and-coming young film actor who'd done his first major role the year before in an indie flick called *Tiger Eyes*. It was now showing on exactly two screens in New York and Los Angeles. While the reviews had been decidedly mixed, his performance as a young man on the psychological edge had been universally lauded.

She'd fought her attraction to him, suspecting his reciprocation was of the wow-she's-poor-and-exotic type that would pass quickly. She was much too proud to go there. Eventually, though, Jonathan convinced her that his feelings for her were real. When he did, she'd opened her heart to him, consequences be damned. It had all nearly blown up in her face when Diane had caught Jonathan and Esme at her guesthouse in a very compromising position. In fact, Esme had nearly been fired. Finally, the decree had come. As Steven had put it, "What you do in the outside world is your own business. But I'd feel more comfortable if the two of you weren't alone on the property." That had been almost five weeks ago. It had taken Jonathan two more weeks to find a vacant apartment in a five-thou-a-month high-rise overlooking the beach in Santa Monica. Esme had already spent two of her rare free nights there.

Ti-Ti finished the song to thunderous applause from the circle of passersby; many of them rushed forward to drop money into his guitar case. "Let's give him some money," Esme urged, digging into her jeans pocket for some singles.

Jonathan stopped her and reached into his back pocket for his wallet. He extracted a crisp fifty-dollar bill and placed it in the guitar case. The musician saw the size of the bill and nodded gratefully.

Jonathan nodded back. "Thanks for the great music, man."

He looped an arm around Esme's shoulders and they headed back down the promenade. It was so strange for Esme to be with a guy so wealthy that donating fifty bucks to a street musician was no big thing. She sighed. Jorge had warned her that she and Jonathan were from two different worlds. It seemed as if every time she turned around, she got a reminder of how right her best friend was.

"Time to finish what we started," Esme told Jonathan after they'd come through the front door of his place. His apartment was on the eleventh floor of a pristine white stone building at Ocean Avenue and Wilshire, easy walking distance to the promenade. With two thousand square feet, two bedrooms, and a huge balcony that looked out toward the Pacific, it was breathtaking. It was also nearly empty. Diane kept begging her stepson to let her ask her favorite designer to swoop in and do the apartment for him, but Jonathan wasn't interested. He'd ordered a top-of-the-line gunmetal king-sized bed and pillow-top Bella mattress over the phone, plus a Claymore billiards table. That was pretty much all he had by way of furnishings.

"That sounds promising." He flicked a light switch. As track lighting illuminated the pool table, he immediately reached for her low-cut apricot T-shirt and started to tug it over her head.

"Brat!" Esme swatted his arm. "That's not what I was talking about."

"Maybe I could change your mind." He gave her a light kiss, which turned hotter when his right hand slid to her butt. "I can be very persuasive."

No kidding, Esme thought, since every inch of her skin screamed *touch me now*.

She loved and hated what he did to her. Loved it because being with him was like every romantic fantasy she'd ever had about how it would feel to be with the perfect boy. Hated it because it gave him power over her.

"Go out on the balcony and wait for me."

"Sex on the balcony? I'm game if you are. Although we could end up on the front page of the *Star.*"

"There's a floodlight out there, right? I have to be able to see."

"See? Ooh. Very kinky."

"Jonathan, think. You've been bugging me for three weeks. You want me to finish the tattoo, don't you?" She punched his bicep lightly where the half-finished tattoo peeked out from the bottom of his short-sleeved tennis shirt. She had been designing a Ferris wheel, because it was on the Ferris wheel at Santa Monica Pier that the two of them had begun to fall for each other. "That half-done thing looks stupid."

His response was to pull off his shirt and throw it onto the pool table. "Finally. Even better than sex!"

"Funny." She also couldn't help but appreciate his naked torso. He was built like the tennis player he was; sculpted muscles, taut washboard abs. "I'll meet you on the balcony. I'm gonna get my stuff." She'd left her tattoo equipment in his kitchen, since the last time she had been there she'd also intended to finish the tattoo. However, passion won out over art. Atop the pool table, in fact.

"Hold on." Jonathan noticed the message light on his phone was blinking. "I've been playing tag with my agent all day. Let me check this."

Esme wandered toward the kitchen as Jonathan pushed a few buttons on his landline and put the whole thing on speaker. "See, no secrets."

"You can have secrets if you want," Esme said, reaching under the sink for the tattooing equipment box that she'd stowed there a couple of days before. Though she would never admit it, she was glad he felt the way he felt. It had to mean, for example, that he wasn't expecting a call from his ex-girlfriend Mackenzie, who was very blond, very rich, and very much on Esme's shit list.

"You have one message," the mechanical voice intoned. "Eight-twenty-three p.m."

A moment later, a harried male voice came on. "Jonathan? Jeff Benson at Paradigm. Sorry to call so late but I was having dinner with Peter Engel. Listen. There've been some interesting developments on *Montgomery*. It's written by the same guys who wrote *Broken Bridges*. The director saw you in *Tiger Eyes*. Anyway, he wants to offer you the role of Josh Parker, no audition, which says a lot about how much he wants you. The money sucks but Laszlo is brilliant and I think you oughta take it. They start shooting in three days, though. Typical last-minute bull, but at least it's local. Anyway, they're messengering over the latest script around three in the morning. Call me when you've read it. First thing."

Jonathan punched the air with excitement, making his muscles ripple again.

"Something good?"

"Something great. I read an early draft. It's amazing—about this town in Alabama and all the eccentric people who live there. Laszlo Cohn is a genius. He had a short nominated for an Oscar. Hot damn!"

"Well, then, congratulations. I hope it's okay if your character has a tattoo."

He took three long strides into the kitchen and lifted her off her feet in a passionate kiss that took her breath away. "Actually, how about if before you finish the tattoo . . ." He nodded toward the billiards table. Oh God. The things he did to her. The way he made her feel.

"Do you ever actually play pool on that thing?" she asked as he kissed her neck.

"I believe in multitasking." His hand gently cupped her right breast.

It took all of Esme's willpower to push him away. Not this time. This time the tattoo would come first, or he'd have a half-finished Ferris wheel on his bicep forever. Besides, he needed to know that she could resist him. She needed to know it even more.

She wriggled out of his embrace and pushed him toward the balcony. "Go."

He complied with a long-suffering sigh. When he was gone, Esme bustled around the kitchen, sterilizing her equipment. Then she ran an extension cord for her tattoo machine from a living room outlet to the exterior before joining him on the balcony. When he was ensconced in a retro redwood lawn chair that his stepmother had delivered as a surprise, she went through the same step-by-step pre-tattoo routine that she did with all her clients: a sterilization procedure involving a massive amount of antiseptic cleanser, the closest shave imaginable to mankind, and then more cleanser. There would be no infection from an Esme Castaneda tattoo.

"Your ex's boys—*cholos,* right?—aren't going to interrupt us?" Jonathan joshed.

Esme grimaced. She'd been in the middle of doing this very tattoo when two of Junior's gangbanger friends had burst through the door of the guesthouse to threaten her and beat up Jonathan. After that incident, it was amazing that he even wanted to be with her. But she wasn't about to admit it.

"Hey, if you get out of line with me, I'll kick your ass myself," she said.

"Tough girl." He smiled up at her.

"Don't try me. I'm the one with the deadly weapons here." She put on her rubber gloves, filled her cups with red, black, and blue ink, and scrutinized the design she'd started on Jonathan's arm more than two months before. She was famous in the barrio for her freehand designs. "Hold still. In case you forgot, this is going to hurt."

The needle bit into his flesh.

"Ouch. Damn!"

"Don't be such a baby," she teased, carefully adding blue ink to the Ferris wheel's spikes. When she stopped to take a break, she realized that she could see the actual Ferris wheel at the Santa Monica Pier out in the distance. It was bathed in yellow light, not more than a half mile from Jonathan's building.

"How's it going?" he asked. " 'Cause my arm is killing me."

"Ten minutes more." She went back to work, crisscrossing lines in red, then black.

It didn't take ten minutes. It took twenty. Finally, though, she was done, and dabbed at the bleeding with bandages and an astringent to cut the blood flow to a bare minimum.

"Okay. That's it." She put down her equipment and stretched, knowing she wasn't done. She still had to wrap his wound, and repeat the instructions about aftercare. Bacitracin, not Neosporin.

He spun around. "Can I see it?"

"Uh-huh. But it'll look a lot better in a few days. And I still have to wrap it." She reached for a small hand mirror that she carried with the rest of her equipment and held it a few feet away from his arm. "Can you see?"

"It's . . ."

"You like it?"

"It's art," he declared. "Art I'll wear forever. It's beautiful, Esme."

She knew that she shouldn't let his words have such an effect on her, but she couldn't help it. It wasn't that she needed a guy's approval to make her feel okay. It was more that he was so sincere. She'd given tattoos to many members of Junior's old gang, Los Locos. They'd all paid her for her work, they'd all been appreciative, but none of them had ever called a tattoo of hers "art."

"Sit back," she told him. "There's more to do. You want a white bandage or cellophane?"

"Cellophane?"

"So your rich friends at the country club can see your Picasso."

His eyes held hers. "Definitely cellophane."

"You might want to wear long sleeves when you go for that film thing."

"Short," he insisted.

The fierceness of his faith in her touched her deeply. She got out her cellophane bandaging and neatly wrapped his upper arm with an airtight barrier.

"So who else is in this new movie?" she asked.

"I think I read something in the *Hollywood Reporter* about Jessica Biel or Mischa Barton as the love interest."

Esme kept her face impassive as she wrapped his bicep.

Those were two very hot, very rich, very white actresses. She wondered if he'd invite her to come visit him on the set. She wondered how she'd feel if she had to watch him do love scenes with Mischa Barton. Most of all, she wondered when she'd be confident enough in her relationship with him to stop all this stupid wondering.

3

Lydia Chandler

Lydia swerved into the driveway of the small house on Twenty-fourth Street in Santa Monica, clicked off KSCR—the closest thing Los Angeles had to an alt station—and turned the key to the green Triumph Spitfire to the Off position. The engine shut down with the peculiar *whiz-whiz-whir* sound it had developed in the last few days, yet another reason for her to return it to the guy who'd loaned it to her.

It was a shame. Returning the Spitfire would leave her car-free, which in Los Angeles was a fate perhaps worse than death. Certainly her measly income as the nanny to Martina and Jimmy—the artificial-insemination offspring of her aunt Kat Carpenter and her Russian wife, Anya Kuriakova—wasn't going to put her behind the wheel of anything besides a used bike any time soon. Yet she had to do what she had to do to assuage her own guilt: Give up the car, and get the guy who had loaned it to her, Luis Amador, out of her life. Even if she had to pay the price in decreased mobility.

Luis was an assistant golf pro at the Brentwood Hills Country Club, the exclusive facility to which the moms—her pet name for her aunt and Anya—belonged. Lydia seemed to spend at least three out of every seven afternoons in their vaunted "Nanny and Me" program, which had been created because so many of the country club members were either working, out on the golf course, or engaging in beauty maintenance at their favorite spas in Beverly Hills (conventional) or Topanga Canyon (alt-type rich).

Lydia and Luis had met one afternoon at the country club. She needed wheels and he had a car that he was willing to lend, but that was not the problem. The problem was that the car transfer evening had turned into a drunken romp up to Malibu, which turned into her awakening the next morning in his bed with both a splitting headache and the loss of her virginity.

When she'd disclosed this little lapse in judgment to her two best friends, Kiley and Esme, they had gone off on her. Not because she'd had sex, but that she couldn't remember if he'd used a condom. Esme had actually accused her of a temporary lapse in sanity. That had been followed by a visit to Planned Parenthood in Echo Park, where she'd been tested for STDs, HIV, and pregnancy. All the tests came back negative, thankfully. She'd need another HIV test in six months, but it seemed as if one night of temporary insanity wasn't going to have lifelong implications.

Still, it irritated Lydia that she'd done something so dumb. It wasn't the virginity thing. Hell, she'd been looking for the perfect male specimen to do the deed ever since she'd arrived in Los Angeles. A red-blooded American girl who had grown up in Amazonia surrounded by naked five-foot-nothing men with rotting teeth who considered it a fashion plus to tie their appendages to their stomachs with twine had to make up for lost time.

This being Los Angeles, it wasn't as if she'd been hard up for candidates. There were plenty of cute guys in Beverly Hills, and she seemed to attract a decent amount of male attention. She was on the tall side, slender, with huge eyes the color of celery and long, choppy, naturally blond hair bleached nearly white by the Amazonian sun. Other girls might fantasize about love, but Lydia fantasized about sex with pretty much everyone she met. She was certain that she'd love sex even more than she loved shopping. All she needed was the right guy.

Then she met Billy Martin. Billy changed everything, and not just because he was six-two, hot, and bore a strong resemblance to Tom Welling from *Smallville*. It was more than that. They got each other. Billy had even lived overseas for many years. He was a design student with an interest in film set design.

As far as Lydia was concerned, all this added up to "Let's Do the Wild Thing Now." But to her great frustration, she had evidently fallen for the most romantic boy on the planet. Lydia's "Let's Do the Wild Thing Now" was Billy's "Let's Really Get to Know Each Other First."

So yes, while she could chalk up her "oops" with Luis to

sexual frustration, she somehow doubted that Billy would see things the same way. Which was exactly why she was not going to tell him.

Luis's battered wooden front door swung open before she could push the white doorbell. "Car trouble? Or was it just that you missed me?"

The front porch light shone on the twinkle in his eyes. Costa Rican by birth, in America on a golf scholarship to Pepperdine, he wore a college golf team shirt and cutoffs not all that different from Lydia's, though hers were by Bebe and originally priced at more than a hundred dollars. She'd found them on sale mismarked a size twelve. With them she wore a lacy silver Anat B. camisole that bared two inches of taut, tanned stomach. Digging up designer wear on a budget was her passion, a passion she was ready to give up as soon as she could banish the B word—"budget"—from her vocabulary. For now, it meant she prowled the boutiques on Melrose and chatted up the sales staff. Sometimes they'd help her with an employee discount.

"It was just so sweet for you to lend me the car," she told him with a trace of her former Texas drawl, and offered him the key on its chain. "But since I don't have a license yet, I don't really think I can use it anymore."

Luis laughed. "That didn't stop you when I offered it to you."

True. She needed a different angle.

"My aunt found out I was driving it and made me bring it back. I have a learner's permit now, but it turns out my driving just sucks," she lied smoothly. "I don't want to wreck it."

He shrugged his broad shoulders. "Wouldn't bother me."

He held the door open. "Want to come in?" He held up a bottle of Guinness beer, half empty. "I've got more of these."

"I can't stay. I have to, you know, work."

He leaned against the doorframe, his eyes flicking over her body. "I been looking for you at the club. Where you been?"

"Oh, you know," she said vaguely.

He raised his eyebrows. "You avoiding me?"

Lydia sighed. She didn't want to hurt the guy—it hadn't been his fault that she was regretting her night with him. On the other hand, she wasn't really a beat-around-the-bush kind of girl, especially having lived in one.

"Luis? Can I level with you?"

"How about," he agreed, folding his arms.

"I'm sure you're a real nice person," she began. "But I've kind of gotten involved with someone in the last few weeks, and that kind of changes things, you know. I'm sure you've been in the same position."

An ambulance racing west on San Vicente blared for a moment, making conversation impossible. Lydia did what she always did when she heard sirens—said a little prayer for whoever was inside. The quality and speed of emergency care in America still amazed her. Back in Amazonia, the Amas had two choices. It was either Lydia's parents and whatever medical supplies had made it up the Rio Negro, or the local shaman.

He smiled. That was a good sign. "That's it?"

"That's it," Lydia assured him. She nodded. "Nothing personal."

"Well, it was a hell of a great night. It's too bad you don't remember it."

She laughed, thinking this was much less difficult than she'd thought it would be. "I'll take your word for it."

"You don't need to be a stranger at the club," he told her. "I don't bite. And if I ever run into you and him together, you've got nothing to worry about."

"Thanks," she told him sincerely. "You're a gentleman, Luis." She looked at her watch, since she'd ordered a cab that was supposed to be arriving any minute. "I've got to go."

He looked past her to the driveway. "You drove here. How are you getting home? Need a ride?"

"Cab. Got it covered."

"Cool. Well, see you at the club sometime. Good luck with this guy, Lydia. I mean it."

Luis closed the door.

Dang. That had been easy. Lydia felt much better. Part of it was that she realized she had not lost her virginity to an asshole. She didn't have to wait five minutes before the yellow cab pulled smoothly up in front of the driveway.

"Where to?" the Pakistani cabdriver asked over blaring music that sounded mysteriously like rutting tapirs in the rain forest.

"Beverly Hills."

"You give me big tip!"

The driver grinned, baring two gold front teeth. As he pulled away, she took one last look back toward the house where she'd lost the virginity she so much wanted to lose, and realized that in five years, ten at the most, she probably wouldn't even remember his name.

Cool.

*　　*　　*

28

"Lydia?"

Damn.

Lydia was hoping to sneak into her guesthouse undetected by either her aunt Kat or her prison warden of a life partner, Anya. Otherwise, she would most certainly be put on emergency duty with the kids.

Martina, especially, had been sleeping poorly of late. For the last two months, Anya had been trying to get her ten-year-old daughter to lose thirty pounds, via a combination of training, diet, and frequent negative-reinforcement pep talks. That any child should be put through such torture struck Lydia as abusive. It wasn't Martina's fault that she looked like a well-developed fifteen. Who could blame her for feeling self-conscious about already having huge breasts? How was such a girl supposed to cope other than by hiding her face behind a curtain of lank brown hair, or directing most of what she said to the ground?

God, Anya was such a bitch. Lydia tried to intervene on Martina's behalf. Just when she began to feel that she was making progress with her cousin's below-zero self-esteem, Momma Anya verbally beat the poor kid down again with her strong Russian accent:

You don't lose weight fast enough, Martina. You have posture of cow, Martina. Where is self-respect, Martina?

Just thinking about it made Lydia grit her teeth. If she didn't need the nanny job so badly, she would have told Anya exactly what she thought of her parenting. That is, it sucked.

"Yeah?" she answered.

Aunt Kat was sitting alone in a deck chair on the stone front porch of the estate, a glass of red wine balanced on one of the armrests and a paperback novel spread cover-up on the other. She wore tennis warm-ups. No longer the competitive player she'd been when she and Anya were younger (the two were former rivals on the women's tour), Kat was now ESPN's chief strategy analyst for all the major tournaments. Another announcer called the matches; Kat explained why they were unfolding as they did.

"Come sit by me." Kat tapped the arm of her deck chair.

"Hey," Lydia said softly. "It's good to have you home."

"I know, I've been traveling like a maniac lately. And the U.S. Open starts in three weeks." She smiled ruefully. "Tennis made my life. Now it's ruining it. Really. Please sit. I want to talk to you."

Something in Lydia's face must have betrayed her fear that she was in trouble again with the moms, because Kat quickly reassured her. "Nothing bad, I promise. It's not about you at all."

"The kids?" Lydia asked as she slid into the empty deck chair next to her aunt.

Kat shook her head, then the two of them sat in silence for a few moments. The night was quiet; the estate was tucked away on one of the winding drives that cut through Beverly Hills. Though there were neighbors to the north and south and across the street, Lydia could barely see any light from their dwellings. They were in the midst of a metropolis of thirteen million people, yet it felt as if they were entirely alone.

"The kids are sleeping," Kat reported.

"Even Martina?"

"Even Martina. If you want some wine, feel free." She indicated the glass on the armrest and frowned. "Anyway, Anya's working so hard to help her. You think she's okay?"

"No. I actually think your daughter is—"

"Not Martina. I meant Anya."

Whoa. Why would her aunt be asking about her partner? Was there a problem? Suddenly, Lydia flashed on something she hadn't thought about in a long time. When Kat was away on business, Lydia had snuck into a closet to "borrow" some clothes from the moms to supplement her meager wardrobe. Under a tall stack of shirts on one of the shelves, she'd come across a copy of the *Kama Sutra* sex guidebook. She'd filched it, of course, and read it cover to cover. Illustrated English-language sex education had limited availability in the rain forest.

The weird thing was that the book was all about heterosexual sex. Why would a lesbian couple want the *Kama Sutra*? Curiosity value? There had to be better gay-themed material somewhere. All it would take was a visit to West Hollywood.

"Come on, Lydia," her aunt cajoled. "We're family here. Just tell me what you think of Anya. What kind of mother she is. Whether she's around here enough when I'm gone. You're not one to hold back."

Then it hit her. Maybe Kat was bi, or at least interested in experimenting. Who could blame her? There was no guy on the planet as butch as Anya.

"She's real . . . efficient," Lydia ventured carefully. The situation struck her as akin to telling an Ama tribesman that his wife was skinny and didn't have droopy breasts—two physical characteristics that deemed you a dog in the Amazon basin.

Even if the Ama had asked your opinion, he'd still use you for curare blow-dart target practice if you didn't insist that his wife was by far the droopiest-breasted babe between the east coast of Peru and the mouth of the Amazon.

Kat rubbed the bridge of her nose, then took another sip of the wine. "It's not fair for me to ask you, Lydia. Anya is your employer too. I know the two of you haven't exactly been buds."

That was an understatement.

"I think we're doing better these last few weeks."

"I think so too, or that's what she tells me. Just the same, Lydia—I'm asking you this as your aunt—if there's anything weird going on with her, anything strange you hear or see, you'll be sure to tell me? Because I travel so much . . . you're kind of like my eyes and ears."

Lydia could almost feel the blow dart penetrate her ass.

She stood. "Fair enough."

"Thanks," Kat told her. "I mean it."

All the way back to her guesthouse, Lydia wondered what had prompted her aunt to wait up for her. It had to be something. The question was: Was it something that Anya had done, or was it something that Kat was suddenly feeling? Dang, what if the moms' marriage was in trouble? As fragile as Martina had been lately, the last thing she needed was divorced mothers. Not only that, what if Anya got custody of the kids? She wouldn't want Kat's niece to be their nanny; she'd probably hire some prison matron and the two of them could bond over torture techniques.

Whatever was wrong, the moms simply had to work it out. For everyone's sake.

4

Kiley screamed.

Serenity screamed.

Then Sid and Platinum screamed too, which made perfect sense, since they were on Colossus, one of the tallest and fastest roller coasters at Six Flags Magic Mountain. There were two drops of more than one hundred feet each, and the coaster reached a speed of over sixty miles an hour. As Kiley looked down at the blur of support beams, the contents of her breakfast gurgled in her stomach. She screamed again. Louder.

The coaster trains rattled along the wooden track, speeding down hill after hill. By now, Serenity was clutching Kiley's left arm so hard that her fingernails were digging a permanent groove into Kiley's bicep, and bellowing that she wanted the ride to stop. Meanwhile, right behind them, Sid and his mother were whooping it up with glee.

"I hate this ride!" Serenity yelled.

"It'll be over! Soon! I hope!" Kiley assured her, wondering if she was going to need stitches for her upper arm.

The roller coaster ripped through its final triple jump, and then slowed to a merciful crawl before it reentered the loading area. "All over," Kiley said in what she hoped was a reassuring voice.

Serenity pulled her talons out of Kiley's arm and brushed the golden hair out of her eyes. "That was cool. Can we go again?"

"I thought you hated it."

"She was so scared she probably wet herself!" Sid hooted gleefully from behind them.

Serenity swung around to accost him. "You're the one who still wets himself, doodyhead!"

This was, in fact, true. Just when Sid had reached the point where he no longer wet the bed at night—a source of great humiliation to him, since he was entering fourth grade in the autumn—Platinum had been arrested. As a result, his nocturnal incontinence had returned with a vengeance.

"I hate you, you suck!" Sid grabbed his little sister's right arm and gave her a rope burn.

"You suck harder, beeotch!" Serenity screamed. "Get off me!"

"Kids, didn't we agree not to use that kind of language anymore?" Kiley reminded them.

"Let 'em be," Platinum insisted as a uniformed park attendant unstrapped them from their seats. "Dr. Fred says they're just angry because the fucked-up legal system took me away from them."

For doing drugs in front of your children, Kiley felt like pointing out, but didn't. Platinum might not be living with her kids right now because she was still awaiting trial—she was installed in a bungalow at the Beverly Hills Hotel, monitored by an ankle bracelet, and under court order not to return to her estate—but she was still Kiley's boss. She could well be calling the shots again one day, and no doubt loved to fire employees as much as ever.

"Free my mom!" Sid yelled, pumping a fist into the air. "Free my mom! Free my mom!"

"Tell it to the cuff, babe," Platinum suggested, as an off-duty cop that the sheriff's department had allowed her to hire for the day moved in to shield her from gawkers. Named Granite, he was red-haired, bearded, and the size of an Appalachian mountain. "The gestapo probably put a microphone in this thing."

Platinum's eyes slid to Ms. Johnson, the court-appointed social worker who was supervising this outing on behalf of the city and county of Los Angeles. "You belong to an oppressed minority," Platinum told the African American woman. "How can you be part of this shit? Don't you have any dignity?"

Ms. Johnson didn't bother to respond. Kiley thought that if Platinum was looking to make a good impression, she was going about it in a rather self-destructive way. That was par for the course. After all, Platinum was Platinum.

Like some sort of strange parade, their group headed for the Freefall Tower at the other side of the park, with Serenity and Sid in the clothing that had been decreed by the colonel for the outing. Before her mother's arrest, Serenity had been allowed to wear junior-hooker designer outfits: bikini tops, tiny low-rise miniskirts, and the tightest of jeans. All that ended with the arrival of the colonel, who did inspection every time the children left the premises.

Today, he had his niece in a crisp cotton sleeveless blue shirt, khaki shorts, and pristine white sneakers. As soon as he was out of sight, though, Serenity found a way to make even this ugly outfit her own, by rolling up and tying the offending shirt just under where her bust would be if she had one, and decorating the sneakers with removable glitter glue.

If the clothes were bad, her hair was worse. Her long, golden waves had been blunt cut to just below her chin. Serenity had cried the whole time she was in the stylist's chair at Supercuts—no more Raymond on Rodeo Drive for her—but the colonel was impervious to her misery. Buck up, he ordered, or he'd take her to the barber at Edwards Air Force Base.

With his mother's departure, Sid had gone through similar agony. He wore khaki shorts identical to his sister's, along with a red tennis shirt. His mop of blond hair had been buzzed off marines-style, his young chest and shoulders noticeably wider because of the push-ups he'd done in response to the colonel's discipline. Unlike his younger sister, he didn't have the heart of a rebel, and never tried to alter his new style.

The colonel had even regulated what Kiley could wear during work hours, which was why she was clad in black trousers and a white shirt, purchased with her new "work uniform" budget. To the colonel, discipline mattered. There was a military-style regime at Platinum's estate; he kept track of merits and demerits on a pocket calculator.

All this horrified Platinum, but there was not a thing she could do about it. It had taken some hard convincing by her high-priced lawyer to convince Judge Ito to grant her a visitation with her children at a public location under the watchful eye of Ms. Johnson.

Platinum even had to have her clothes approved. Instead of, say, Badgley Mischka capris and a white Imitation of Christ tank top with Bottega Veneta Noce Super Spiga natural linen sandals, Ms. Johnson mandated de rigueur don't-notice-me threads: jeans, Chicago Cubs baseball cap, sunglasses, and a plain white men's dress shirt. So far, no one had noticed her presence.

As they strolled past the park midway, though, a tall model-thin girl in a Notre Dame High School varsity volleyball T-shirt, approaching from the opposite direction with a group of equally thin friends, stabbed a finger in their direction.

"Omigod!" she bellowed at a volume that could certainly be heard in eastern Nevada. "It's Platinum!"

Like a pack of zombies zooming in on fresh human meat, she and her teammates rushed forward, shouting Platinum's name, begging for autographs. Pieces of paper, pens, and lip pencils suddenly materialized in outstretched hands. The bodyguard and Ms. Johnson tried to step in front of Platinum to fend them off, but it was too late.

Other park guests overheard the name Platinum and joined in the ruckus. Within a few seconds, there were no fewer than fifty people clustered around the rock star. The fact that the object of their affections had recently been arrested for endangering her children and had suffered the ignominy of being re-moved from her own home seemed not to matter a whit. Such was Platinum's star power.

"Back away, back away," Granite ordered.

"Omigod, I'm like your biggest fan!" A fat middle-aged woman wearing a button that pledged her allegiance to Toby Keith pushed to the front of the circle, all three of her chins jiggling in ecstasy. She managed to thrust a gas station receipt and pencil stub at Platinum, avoiding Granite's beefy arm.

"Thanks," Platinum replied, scribbling her name and hand-ing it back. Cameras and cell-cameras were clicking away. Plat-inum posed, shoulders back, chest out, tossing her trademark silvery hair over one eye.

"You the bomb, girl!" a Latina yelled from the back of the mob. "What they did to you is a crime!"

Others in the crowd agreed enthusiastically. Kiley looked over at Ms. Johnson, who now had her hands on her hips and eyes narrowed.

"Not guilty!" A spontaneous chant erupted. "Not guilty! Not guilty!"

Platinum grinned wildly as the onlookers joined in with enthusiasm. "Thanks for your support. I'll have my day in court!"

Ms. Johnson stepped in. "We need to ratchet this down some," she announced, but Platinum ignored her, blowing kisses to her fans and taking her grinning children under her arms.

"Clear out!" Granite yelled.

"Go!" Platinum told her admirers. "See you at the concert stage in a half hour! I'm singing!"

* * *

"Please welcome to the Magic Mountain main stage a very special surprise guest for the day. Ladies and gentlemen, the one and only . . . Platinum!"

A huge crowd had gathered. The people went wild, screaming, whistling, and clapping. Kiley stood just offstage with Ms. Johnson, Granite, and both kids. She watched as the leader of the Magic Mountain house band motioned to the wings. With professional aplomb, Platinum confidently strode to the mike and shook the clean-cut young man's hand.

"I'm not sure I should have allowed this," Ms. Johnson groused. "Look at all these people."

Once the park public address system had announced that Platinum was going to be performing a few songs in concert right here at Magic Mountain, it seemed as if every one of the thousands of guests visiting the park had flocked to the main stage circle, which only had enough wooden benches to seat several hundred. Most people came to Magic Mountain to ride the coasters like X and SCREAM!, not to listen to a glorified lounge act or watch one of the high school or amateur dance troupes take their moment in the sun. Platinum, though, was a big attraction, all the more so because of her recent notoriety.

"I think it's good for the kids," Kiley said carefully. "It'll make them proud of their mom. Just look at them."

Serenity and Sid stood together just to her left, their faces shining with pride.

"Maybe," Ms. Johnson agreed. "But this is highly irregular."

There had, in fact, been a heated impromptu conference when Platinum had announced that she'd be singing at the Magic Mountain main stage. It turned out that she had called the park ahead of time and gotten permission to perform, so long as her minders were in agreement. Platinum played the it's-good-for-my-children card heavily, and a reluctant Ms. Johnson acquiesced, threatening to cut off the microphone and return Platinum straight to Judge Ito if there were any missteps.

Platinum had to wait a moment or two for the cheers to die down.

"Hello, Magic Mountain!" Her voice boomed through the public address system. "It's great to be here. Ready for some music?"

Platinum turned to the five-piece band that looked as if it had just collectively died and gone to rock-and-roll heaven, shouted some instructions, then whipped back around and launched into her first hit, "Eighth-Grade Roadkill."

> *"I'm eighth-grade roadkill*
> *Don't matter I got other skills*
> *Not reading and writin'*
> *Mostly chillin' or fightin'*
> *Eighth grade is a kind of hell*
> *Parents don't know so well*
> *I'm eighth-grade roadkill*
> *Now wha-choo got to say?"*

Platinum started pogoing around the stage while she sang—the transformation she made as a performer was re-markable, and she was in great shape for a woman well into her forties. Any other woman that age would have looked ridiculous. Platinum, though, just looked cool.

She brought that song to a close, and then raced through a four-song medley of her biggest hits: "Love Junkie," "Eat Your Heart Out," "More and More and More," and "Who's Your Daddy?" This last one, Kiley knew, had been composed just a few years ago as a kind of answer song to all the queries Platinum got about the paternity of her children. She never answered that question, and the song lyrics underscored her intent never to tell.

"Who's Your Daddy?" finished to thunderous applause and whistles from the crowd.

Serenity was literally jumping up and down with glee. "That's my mom! That's my mom!"

"Talented lady, for sure," the social worker muttered to Kiley. "If she could ever get her head screwed on right." She gave a signal to Platinum that this would be her last song. Platinum made the okay sign to show that she understood.

"I'm here with two very special guests today," Platinum told the crowd. "The most special people in the world. Friends, I'd like you to meet my two youngest children, Serenity and Siddhartha. Guys, come on out and take a bow!"

Once they got an approving nod from Ms. Johnson, Serenity and Sid charged out to their mom; the little girl blew kisses to the crowd as it cheered. Except for the clothes, she was a miniature of her mother, with an equal amount of moxie.

The singer put her arms around her children. "Some of you might know my family's had a difficult time lately. I've had a lot of time to just think. And write. I want you guys to hear a new song I wrote. It's called 'I Don't Know.' I don't know what the future is going to bring. But I do know if any of you are moms or dads out there, love your children. And kids, show your moms and dads that you love them back.

> *"I don't know about tomorrow*
> *I just know about today*
> *There's no crystal ball to search in*
> *That can show you the right way*
>
> *"All I know is what we have*
> *And what we have got is love*
> *It's a gift to every one of us*
> *That comes from up above*
>
> *"I don't know about next week*
> *I don't know about next year*
> *I don't know if it will bring us peace*
> *Or war or joy or fear*
>
> *"All I know is what we have*
> *And what we have got is love*
> *It's a gift to every one of us*
> *That comes from up above*
>
> *"We've got love."*

Kiley looked out at the crowd as Platinum sang this very un-Platinum-like song. People's eyes were shining; parents with arms around their children were swaying to the melody.

This was a Platinum she'd never seen before. Hokey or not,

contrived or not, Machiavellian or not—Kiley was not so naive that she didn't see the PR benefits of a song and performance like this—it was still a touching moment. Impressive, in fact. If this was the new Platinum, maybe she needed to be arrested more often.

5

Esme contemplated her reflection in the bathroom mirror as she quickly pulled her hair back in a ponytail for a no-nonsense nanny look. At least that was what she'd hoped for. Diane had given her the morning off because Easton and Weston were seeing their English-language coach, a multilingual professor at USC who made extra money removing the accents of those who immigrated. Though Esme had assured Diane that the twins would sound completely American in a matter of months, the anxious mother wasn't taking any chances.

Even with the twins away, Diane asked Esme to come up to the house. There was something she wanted to discuss. Esme was puzzled, since things had been going really well lately; she'd even been given a raise. She hoped it wasn't about Jonathan. Their most recent night together, after she finished his tattoo, they'd celebrated his potential new movie role with Taittinger champagne, chocolate-covered strawberries, and fresh mango. After that . . . well, remembering the "after that" part was what made her blush. They'd awakened on the pool table. Enough said.

As she hurried up the gravel path to the main house, past the swings and sandbox where she had first met Easton and Weston, past the tennis court where she had first seen Jonathan hitting balls with Mackenzie, she vowed to banish thoughts of that night from her mind.

Steven and Diane Goldhagen's Bel Air mansion was in a class by itself in a city that sprouted mansions like dunghills sprouted mushrooms. Three floors and thirty rooms, it was constructed of natural wood, with soaring windows and radically sloped roofs. A series of cascading reflecting pools that produced a constant lulling white noise lined one side and circled around to the front.

Esme approached it from the back, pulling open the heavy, gleaming brass door handle and then making her way through the enormous front hallway with its twenty-foot ceiling toward the family room. This room was a marvel. Half open-air and half roofed, it could be closed off completely in the rare case of inclement weather. There was a freestanding stone fireplace surrounded by a riot of flowers that were changed every other day by the local Conroy's floral shop.

She found Diane already waiting. Esme guessed that her employer was a good fifteen years younger than her husband of two years. The embodiment of a Hollywood cliché, she was Steven's second wife, upgraded from being a line producer on one of his many successful shows. Since they married, she'd quit working, preferring to devote her time to her hair, makeup, and body, plus any number of worthy charities. Today she wore a Louis Vuitton cotton and silk taupe jacket with gold piping, and skinny jeans. Her champagne-colored toy poodle, Cleo, whose look changed as often as Diane's, sat by her feet. For today, the Beverly Hills Mutt Club—the designer canine boutique on Santa Monica Boulevard—had outfitted the poodle in a gold lamé doggie sweater with a gold neck ribbon, plus matching glittery gold polish on Cleo's perfectly manicured nails. As a BHMC member, Cleo also received regular doggie massages and a "communication session" with Kim Ogden-Avrutik, famous for her ability to speak with canines.

"Hey, Esme." Steven strode into the room, a very different picture from his wife. His friendly, tanned face was lined, since he was successful enough in Hollywood to eschew Botox without economic repercussions. A baseball cap hid his thinning hair, and he was sporting his on-again-off-again scraggly beard. If you didn't know that he was one of the most successful producers in the history of television, you could easily mistake him for a homeless guy outside the Staples Center. "How's life?"

"Fine," Esme replied, resisting the urge to add "sir." Mr. Goldhagen had told her endless times to call him Steven, but it still felt odd.

"Sit, sit." Steven motioned toward a high-backed eggshell velvet chair. Meanwhile, he joined Diane on the matching sofa. Okay, this was getting stranger by the moment. As easygoing as Steven was, he was almost always working. Even when he ran on his home-office treadmill (he had another in his new digs on the Warner Brothers lot, where he'd recently inked a three-year deal), he used the time to watch daily rushes from one of his shows. What was he doing home on a workday?

"We have a surprise for you," Diane said. Cleo barked her

agreement, which made Diane laugh. "I think it will make you really happy."

You're doubling my salary, Esme guessed silently as she waited for the kicker. *You bought a winning lottery ticket and since you're already richer than God you've decided to give the fifty-five mil to my parents so they don't have to scrub your toilets and mow your lawn and nice you to death.*

Yeah. Like *that* was going to happen.

"You are about to take a trip to the airport." Diane scratched Cleo's neck under the gold ribbon.

She was picking someone up for them. Why? They had one full-time driver and a part-time fill-in.

"Remember when we were in Jamaica and the girls wandered off at that festival?" Steven recalled. "And you met a lovely young woman named Tarshea, who helped you find them?"

Esme's heart quickened. She did remember. Tarshea Manley was a tall, lithe, and beautiful Jamaican girl, a couple of years older than Esme. They'd met when Tarshea painted the twins' faces during a visit to the sugarcane cutting festival on Jamaica's southern shore. One minute, Esme had been chatting with Tarshea about the girl's desire to go to art school and how impossible that goal was in a place like Jamaica. The next moment, the twins were gone. Esme couldn't remember a time when she'd been more panicked over something that was her direct responsibility.

It was Tarshea who had helped her find the girls and then covered for Esme, pretending she had glanced away from them to look for another color of face paint. Tarshea's story was the only reason Diane and Steven had not fired Esme on the spot. She had been so grateful that she'd asked the Gold-hagens if they could help bring Tarshea to America and fulfill her dream of going to art school. Maybe she could find a nanny job. Maybe Esme and her friends could help her on that score.

Steven had jotted down Tarshea's contact information, which consisted of her minister's phone number. Tarshea's family, like so many others in Jamaica, was too poor to own a phone. Esme had seen the look on her beautiful face when they'd departed to go back to their exclusive resort on the north side of the island; the sadness and resignation. Esme could tell just what the Jamaican girl was thinking: the rich Americans would have her out of mind just as soon as she was out of sight.

Now they were bringing up Tarshea's name. And the airport. So could it possibly mean—

"We managed to secure Tarshea a work visa," Steven continued. "We hope that's a good surprise."

"It's . . . fantastic!" Esme cried. "You never said anything . . . I can't believe . . . when did you . . ." She knew she was sputtering but she couldn't help herself.

Diane nodded approvingly. "We weren't sure we could pull it off. That's why we didn't tell you ahead of time. And we don't have a nanny job lined up for her yet, so we stretched the truth and said she'd be working for us. I hope you don't mind sharing your guesthouse with her while we find her another position."

"No, no, of course not! Of course it's fine. I can't believe the two of you did this. It's so . . . kind."

Steven looked fondly at his beautiful wife. "Thank Diane. It was her idea. She was pretty damn relentless about it."

"Thank you," Esme told Diane, and meant it with all her heart. Diane was such an enigma. She was high-strung and high-maintenance, worried about appearances, and at times utterly superficial. Then she turned around and did something like this.

"Tarshea's minister went on and on about how wonderful a girl she is, and how talented," Diane said. "So I registered her for art classes at the Museum of Contemporary Art starting in the fall. My friend Abigail Huff is a docent."

Steven glanced at his classic Rolex tank watch. "Tarshea's flight from Kingston arrives at LAX in ninety minutes. You'd better get going. International arrivals building. You'll see her when she clears customs."

"Great. Let me get my keys."

Esme jumped up. She'd need to run back to the guesthouse to get her purse and the keys to the Goldhagens' Audi, the car her employers had provided for her daily use.

Diane waved her off. "No need. Stuart will drive the limo. We thought Tarshea would enjoy arriving in America in style."

"That's right. And after that, he'll take you to the Warner Brothers commissary for lunch, over in Burbank. The good one at the office building on Riverside, not the bullshit one on the lot. All you need to do is sign when you go past the cashier. See if your nanny friends can join you—what are their names? Lydia and Kiley? I'll call their bosses and send temps to watch their kids if they want. Tarshea needs to meet some people." Steven got out his BlackBerry. "I'll call the commissary now."

"That's very generous of you," Esme told him.

Steven rubbed his chin thoughtfully. "Just following your lead, Esme. If it wasn't for you and the initiative you took, Tarshea wouldn't be coming here. I think it's the very least that Diane and I can do."

Tarshea stared wide-eyed out the rear window of the black stretch limousine as it inched north on the 405 freeway somewhere south of Marina del Rey. Though it wasn't yet noontime, they were stuck in traffic, with cars and SUVs in both directions as far as the eye could see.

"So many cars," Tarshea murmured in her lilting Jamaican accent. "This is the third time in my life I've ever been in a private car. Only buses for this Jamaican girl. No wonder none of this seems real."

Esme smiled, thinking what a huge culture shock this had to be for Tarshea, who had arrived with but a single beige suitcase held together with gray duct tape. She wore a much-washed plain white cotton blouse primly buttoned to her chin, and a thin navy blue polyester skirt that fell to her slim calves. On her feet were cheap navy blue patent leather flats. Her hair was slicked back in a short braid that showed off an elegant, swanlike neck. There was a small gold cross around her neck; her face bore no makeup.

"I didn't think this would really happen," Tarshea confessed. "I don't know how to thank you."

"I didn't do it. Diane Goldhagen did. Thank her."

"You are lucky to work for such an admirable woman; adopting the twins, taking me in. . . . So tell me, how are the girls?"

50

"Fine, funny, spoiled rotten. Turning into Americans before my eyes."

Esme loved Easton and Weston dearly. They were both still happily experiencing so many things they hadn't had back in Colombia. Everything from escalators to ice makers to cable television fascinated them. On the other hand, after barely more than two months in America, they were starting to act as though they were entitled to the life they'd parachuted into out of the blue. Recently, Jonathan and Esme had taken them out for their favorite food in the world—ice cream. When told that Cold Stone Creamery was temporarily sold out of their favorite, chocolate-chocolate-chip, each had a meltdown right in front of the counter.

"They should always remember where they came from," Tarshea said.

"Well, Steven and Diane don't necessarily see it that way."

"I don't understand."

Esme tented her fingers. This was a subject that got her angry. First, the children had been born with very nice Spanish names—Isabella and Juana—but Diane had changed them to the more Hollywood-friendly Easton and Weston. Then, in a city full of Spanish speakers and Hispanic culture, it seemed more and more as though Steven and Diane were shielding their daughters from their roots. Yes, they'd hired bilingual Esme as the nanny, but that was to ease the twins' transition to America. In Esme's opinion, the Goldhagens could be in for a rude awakening when the girls got older and realized how little their adoptive parents had made of their root culture.

"Me placeré verlos otra vez," Tarshea recited in halting Spanish as Stuart the driver inched the limo forward. They saw

the reason for the traffic jam: A BMW had tangled with a Hummer in the right-hand lane. The Hummer had won, judging from the condition of the Beemer's rear end. "Did I say it right?"

Esme was astonished. " 'I will be happy to see them again.' When did you learn Spanish?"

"When my minister told me that he'd spoken with Mrs. Goldhagen, that she was arranging a visa for me, I immediately took a book from his library. I thought it would be important to speak to the girls in their first language. I hope my accent is not too atrocious."

How nice was this girl? And how thoughtful?

"That's so sweet of you! Maybe together we can help them remember where they came from." Spontaneously, she reached out and touched Tarshea's slender forearm. "I'm so glad you're here."

Tarshea looked troubled. "You don't mind that I will be sharing your house? That is what Diane told my minister. Not that you'd be surprised, but that we'd be sharing."

"Not at all. It will be fun."

"I want you to know, Esme, that until I get a job, I will help you every way that I can," Tarshea declared. "I can take care of the girls for you any time you want."

Esme was touched. "Thanks."

"You are more than welcome. If I lived two lifetimes, I could not do enough to pay you back."

"I told you," Esme insisted, "Diane is the one who—"

"But it was you who gave her the idea," Tarshea pointed out. "I love Jamaica. It's my home. But . . ." Her eyes flicked back to the window. "You are an American. So you don't know what it's like. To feel that you are stuck in poverty, to feel that no matter what you do, you can do nothing to change your circumstances."

How ironic. Tarshea assumed that because Esme was American she was at least modestly wealthy herself. That doors were open to her. That anything was possible, when the truth was that Esme had more in common with the Jamaican girl than she did with the Goldhagens.

"Is their home very beautiful?" Tarshea asked eagerly.

Esme laughed. "That's an understatement."

"My home is two rooms," Tarshea explained. "For me, my parents, my two sisters and brother. We must go down to the well for water. Our bathroom we share with six other families. It is a ways from our house."

God. Esme couldn't even imagine that.

"At the Goldhagens' at my—*our*—guesthouse, we have our own bathroom and it's gorgeous. You'll have your own bedroom. And I'll introduce you to my friends. We're going to meet them for lunch now, in fact. Over at a movie studio. Warner Brothers."

Tears literally came to Tarshea's eyes. "I cannot imagine."

"Well, whatever you could imagine, the reality is even better."

They finally passed the mess of the collision and started to speed up. Tarshea shook her head. "It's a dream. . . ."

Esme smiled, thrilled for her new friend. "No. It's real. Your dream is about to come true."

6

Kiley stood on line with the three other girls at the entrance to the bustling commissary on the ground floor of the Warner Brothers office building on Riverside Drive. Located outside the main studio compound, the building held the writers' offices of many WB Studios shows, including Steven's new one about the medical interns. Though the new TV season was still six weeks away, everything was in full production, which meant the commissary was jammed with workers.

Instead of playing spot-the-celebrity, Kiley's eyes were on Tarshea, who looked both overjoyed and bewildered. It wasn't surprising, since Tarshea had told them much about her life in Jamaica on the ride from Bel Air to Burbank.

What would it be like to get on a plane in that world and land in this one, where a chauffeured limousine picked you up at the airport, where you rode through streets and boulevards lined with mansions and ended up at lunch at a famous studio commissary with three American girls? It had to be over-whelming.

"This is . . . it's . . ." Tarshea couldn't seem to find any words.

"Usually we just eat with our kids," Kiley told her, lest the girl think that a midday reprieve like this was a daily thing.

"You'll be amazed how quick you can get used to living the high life," Lydia added.

"I—I don't know . . . ," Tarshea stammered.

Esme touched her arm. "Hey, it's okay."

Kiley nodded. "You're with three friends now."

Two gorgeous, skinny girls—one blond, one brunette—strode past them. Each had long, straight hair gleaming with highlights. The blonde wore a tiny yellow plaid stretch-cotton skirt, a tangerine tank, and snakeskin cowboy boots. The brunette was in Lucky Brand denim capris, a shrunken pink lace jacket, and rhinestone flip-flops. Laminated Warner Brothers picture IDs hung around their necks.

Their eyes flicked disdainfully at Tarshea, and then away.

Tarshea smoothed her cheap skirt self-consciously. "My clothes . . ."

"Your clothes are fine," Esme reassured her.

Tarshea didn't look convinced. Kiley didn't blame her. There was a difference between dressed-like-you've-fallen-out-of-bed and threadbare. She, Esme, and Lydia were all wearing variations on the jeans/tank top/T-shirt/work shirt thing. Yet everything was new enough to fit in. Not like the Jamaican girl.

"Her clothes are *not* fine and we all know it," Lydia corrected. "Let's just call an ugly ol' outfit like it is." She looped an arm through Tarshea's. "But not to worry, sweet pea. Until recently I had to machete my own fashions. We'll burn what you're wearing and get you all new stuff. Shopping is one of my life talents."

Kiley found this comment amazingly insensitive. Undoubtedly Tarshea was broke. She couldn't afford to shop, especially not at any store that Lydia would deem shopworthy.

Finally, the line moved ahead enough for them to get close to the food. "So what do I do, Esme?" Tarshea asked hesitantly.

"Get in any of the lines." Esme pointed to a half dozen stations to their left. "There's a pasta line—you can pick from like six different kinds of pasta and then invent your own sauce. Then there's two hot food areas—the daily specials are on that whiteboard over there. And in the center of the room is a giant salad bar so you can make your own salad. Forget about the price. Steven and Diane are paying."

Tarshea nodded, but her eyes seemed wary.

"After you get what you want, go to the cashier. She'll ring everything up, and I'll sign for it. The seats are through that passageway to the right. Simple."

"I wish my family could see this. All this food!" Tarshea shook her head in wonderment. "Okay. No problem, mon. I'll just follow you all, if you don't mind."

They opted for pasta. After Kiley ordered penne with garlic, butter, anchovy paste, and freshly grated Parmesan, Tarshea said she'd have the same. Then they built themselves huge spinach and mushroom salads, picked up drinks, and finally got in line for the cashier. When they went through, Esme simply signed for all the food.

"Hello! Vacating at two o'clock," Kiley called. She cocked her head toward a round table to her right where four guys in suits stood up to leave.

"Agents," Lydia said knowingly, as one of the suits caught her eye and gave her the kind of appreciative male look that Lydia always seemed to generate. "They're the only ones who ever wear suits."

"How do you know?" Kiley wondered.

"I read it in *Entertainment Weekly*," Lydia replied, brushing her choppy hair off her face. She unwrapped her straw and stuck it into her bottle of Dasani Raspberry just as Kiley's cell rang.

She fished in her jeans for her cell. The call was from her home in La Crosse—the number was right there on caller ID. "Hello?"

"Kiley, sweetie . . . it's your mother."

"Hi, Mom!"

"How are you?"

Kiley could barely hear her. "Just a sec, I'm going to find someplace quieter to talk. I'm at the Warners commissary. It's a madhouse."

"I'll hold on."

Kiley excused herself, but not before Lydia threatened to finish both their lunches if she wasn't back soon. Through the window, she saw a broad exterior patio where people were standing around either smoking or talking on their cells. A moment or two later, she was out there too, leaning against a large concrete planter that held a profusion of pansies.

"I'm here, Mom."

"How are you? How's every little thing? How are things at that rock star's house?"

"Fine, Mom. Her brother-in-law is still in charge."

"That's good. He seems like a very nice man."

There was a large electronic clock inside the glass doors that led to the main entrance of the building; Kiley saw that it was 1:11 p.m. "Hey, what are you doing calling me from home? Shouldn't you be at the Derby?"

"Umm . . . yes. I guess I should," her mother admitted. "This has been a hard day for me. Two prisoners escaped from the prison in Chippewa Falls."

Kiley groaned inwardly as she figured out why her mother had called her. She'd had a panic attack because of these escaped prisoners. It had been so bad she couldn't even bring herself to go to work. She'd be trapped at home watching the news until the men were captured.

Kiley couldn't imagine what it would be like to live like that. Or to be her mom. So horrible. The worst thing in the world.

"Mom?" Kiley tried to be reassuring. Now was not the time to come down on her mom. "It's okay. I'm glad you called me. Do you feel safe in the house?"

"Yes."

"Then don't go out. I'm sure you have plenty of sick days saved up."

"I do."

"Then you did the right thing." Kiley was adamant, knowing that was what her mother needed to hear. In the middle of her mom's panic attacks, often Kiley was the only person who could keep her on the right side of sanity. "You call me if you need me, okay?"

"Okay, Kiley." Her mother's voice sounded like a child's, which gave Kiley the uneasy sensation of being a mother to her own mother. "I'm going to watch the news again."

"Bye, Mom. Call me if you need me," Kiley repeated.

She heard her mother hang up, and snapped her cell shut, feeling very sad.

A few minutes later, Kiley was back at the table in the commissary, coming in on a conversation about finding Tarshea a job. Fortunately, Lydia had left her lunch intact, so she dug into her pasta.

"So Tarshea, we need to find you a job, right?"

"I am hoping to find one, yes," Tarshea said shyly. She sat very straight and smoothed her napkin on her lap. "I hope that Esme's employers can help me, too."

"But like I told you, Tarshea is an artist," Esme put in, forking some angel hair pasta into her mouth. "She wants to go to art school."

"Well, I want to have sex with Orlando Bloom, but that's not gonna happen overnight, either," Lydia quipped.

Kiley rolled her eyes. Evidently Lydia's cheating-on-Billy-that-didn't-count-because-she-was-drunk hadn't taught her much about fidelity.

"Oh, wipe that look off your face," Lydia told Kiley with a chuckle. "I'm joking. Unless, of course, I happen to meet Orlando and then I might have to let nature take its course. Back to you, Tarshea. A game plan is in order. Once upon a time, the three of us wanted to run a nanny placement service. But it was more trouble than it was worth. So maybe we should just get you poached at the country club."

"Poached . . . like an egg?" Tarshea ventured.

"Not exactly." Esme gave her a brief explanation of the concept of nanny poaching at the country club, but Tarshea didn't look as if she was tracking.

"How about if we give Tarshea a few days to settle in?" Kiley suggested. "Everything must be so new and strange."

Tarshea speared a spinach leaf and chewed it thoughtfully. "In a way yes, but in a way no. It is new in my own experience but I've seen it on television. We get all the American shows. Also some from Cuba."

"Don't think most Americans live like this," Esme advised.

Tarshea smiled. "You three do."

"Only because we work for rich people." Kiley bit into the pasta. It was heavenly—as good as anything she'd eaten anywhere in Los Angeles.

"In that case, I think I would like to work for rich people very—Jesus, Mary and Joseph!" Tarshea gasped, then peered obviously across the room. "*Coo yah! Is that Tom Welling?*"

Kiley followed Tarshea's gaze. A tall, incredibly handsome guy with dark brown hair and a day's worth of stubble on his chin was deep in conversation with a beautiful, petite woman with Asian features.

"I think so," Esme said. "The *Smallville* offices are here. He might be in for meetings."

"That is my favorite show!" Tarshea exclaimed. "All my friends, we all meet to watch it on our church TV."

"Dang, no wonder everyone says that Billy looks like him," Lydia commented, checking Tom out in person. He was sitting down to eat with an older woman, probably a reporter. "Billy's my boyfriend," she added for Tarshea's benefit.

Tarshea was in a state of shock. "I am in the same room as Tom Welling. Everything cook and curry!"

"Everything cook and . . . ?" Kiley raised her eyebrows.

Tarshea grinned. "Just an expression from Jamaica. It means everything is just great."

Lydia sipped her drink. "Oh, there're all kinds of stars in here. I saw Alexis Bledel over at the salad bar. You know, from *Gilmore Girls*? And the cute guys from *E.R.* were ahead of us at the cashier. The white guy is Shane West and the hot black guy is Mekhi Phifer."

"How do you know these things?" Kiley wondered.

"*Entertainment Weekly*," Esme guessed.

"Nope. The *Star*."

Tarshea shook her head. "So much . . . so much *everything*." She picked up her fork, but then put it down again; her plate of pasta was still untouched. "I have a friend from church, Marie—she is a social director at one of the large resorts. That is a job everyone wants but they are impossible to get unless you are very well connected. She told me stories about the rich Americans at the resort, how they look, what they wear, how they act . . . and I thought . . . America can't be like that, really."

"It isn't," Esme insisted.

"But Esme," Tarshea objected. "Just look around. For some people, it really is."

"Y'all, there is nothing noble about poverty." Lydia hoisted her empty bottle into the air. "So here's to all of us becoming filthy rich."

Kiley hesitated to raise her bottle, and noticed that Esme wasn't quick to join the toast, either. The whole thing was more complicated than that. Money was important, yes. But she'd take her own messed-up lower-middle-class family over Platinum's super-messed-up rich one any day of the week.

She never got the chance to say any of that. Because before she could object, Tarshea was raising her bottle to Lydia. "Yah, mon. Filthy rich. I like the sound of that. With streets that are paved with gold."

"And boyfriends that make other girls drool, and designer wardrobes to die for." Lydia grinned at Tarshea and clinked their bottles together. "Welcome to America."

7

"I have blond hair and blue eyes. My mom is a famus fashion designer who is very pretty and my dad is a famus heart surgeen like the ones you see on TV. I don't want to brag too bad but I am very popular and not just because we are very rich. My friends say I am very cute and skinny and petite. I don't say that even if it's true because it would be stuck-up. Remember that modeling job I told you about that I did with Dakota Fanning? It was so fun. We both love modeling—"

"What are you doing?"

Martina jumped and tried to use her computer mouse to position the cursor so that she could erase the e-mail she'd been writing. It was too late, though. Lydia had already read it over her shoulder.

"Nothing."

Lydia sat on the edge of the girl's bed closest to her desk. "You know you can tell me, sweet pea."

Martina shook her head and stared at her plush wall-to-wall pale pink carpeting.

"Some kind of story?" Lydia prompted.

"You'll tell," Martina whispered. She peeked through her veil of dank hair. "You'll tell Momma Anya. I'm already in trouble with her."

"About what?"

"It doesn't matter."

It could be one of a dozen things. From the moment that Lydia joined Aunt Kat and her partner, Anya had ridden Martina mercilessly. Most recently, she'd put her chunky daughter on a food and exercise plan worthy of the Dallas Cowboys training camp. Every morning, Lydia would come to breakfast to find a detailed note ordering the food that Martina was permitted to eat and the physical activities that she had to do under Lydia's watchful eye.

Yes, the girl was in better shape than before, but she had been blessed by God with one of those frames that exercise made stronger instead of slimmer. She still hid her body under the baggiest clothes she could find.

"No I won't, baby girl," Lydia insisted. She tipped Martina's chin upward so that their eyes met. "You know I don't lie to you, right?"

Martina nodded, but looked miserable. "There's a boy."

Martina had met a boy? When? And where? Oh no. What if it was one of those Internet things? A girl like Martina would drop into a load of crap faster than a wild boar into a deadfall.

"What boy?"

"Kevin. His name is Kevin."

"Kevin who?"

"Covington." Martina bit at a fingernail that had already been nibbled into near nonexistence. "Well, see, he's going to my school in the fall. He moved here from England."

That was a relief. At least he was a real kid her age.

"When did you meet him?"

Martina bit her lower lip. "I kind of didn't. Remember when that letter came from Crossroads about fifth grade next year and Momma Anya told you to open it and report back to her but you never did?"

Oops. Now that Martina mentioned it . . . Lydia had left the letter on Martina's dresser and forgotten all about it. She'd have to tend to that later.

"I kind of read it too. Don't be mad."

"I'm not, sweetie," Lydia assured her, sneaking a glance at the Hello Kitty clock on the pink far wall. Already ten o'clock. Though she'd had a relatively easy day the day before when she'd met that girl Tarshea for lunch at the Warners lot, this particular Wednesday was shaping up to be a bear. Lydia still had to get Martina through her computer Russian lesson (Anya would test her), out to the tennis court for her hitting session with the pro (who would write a formal progress report), and then make sure that Martina ate her healthy and nutritious four-hundred-calorie lunch. Though the moms' new chef, Paisley, was talented, it was impossible for even her to make tofu, romaine salad without dressing, one quarter cup of brown rice, and organic apple slices taste decent.

The afternoon would be no better. There was an Anya-generated list of activities for Martina a mile long, including an hour-long aerobic workout. As least she didn't have to worry about Jimmy, who was at the country club with Kat.

"Well, see, the letter said this boy was starting in our class in the fall," Martina went on. "And it said he wanted e-mail buddies before he comes and it gave his e-mail address and stuff. So I wrote to him and he wrote back."

Oh, so that was what this was all about. Very innocent. Except for the minor detail that when Kevin what's-his-name showed up at Martina's school in four weeks, he was going to find that nothing she'd written to him was the truth.

Fair enough, Lydia thought. Four weeks to repair the damage.

"Let's get to your Russian," Lydia suggested. "You don't want to be late for tennis."

"Yes I do."

Lydia contemplated bribing the tennis pro so that Martina could skip it. She doubted that it would work, though. The tennis pro was Anya's close, personal friend, meaning she was in the gay sports mafia, a closed-circuit world of top lesbian athletes who dated, mated, and recreated together, and even occasionally procreated with the assistance of modern medical science. A hetero nanny didn't stand a chance against that.

"Well, how about if we come back and finish the Russian this afternoon after your workout? We have a half hour before tennis. We can do whatever you want to—"

Her cell rang. She extracted it from the back pocket of a pair of white Seven skinny-legged jeans she'd rummaged from the lost-and-found at the country club.

"Yeah?"

"Hey, Lydia, Billy."

Billy. She loved the deep sound of his voice. It did things to her. Things she'd rather have done by him in person, and soon, the better to erase Luis from her memory.

"Hey, Billy," she greeted him, holding up a "just a sec" finger to Martina. "What's up?"

"I saw a beautiful woman walk by a few minutes ago in the most amazing sari," he explained. "Violet and red—right out of a Picasso—gave me quite a hankering for some Indian food. You up for it?"

Lydia had to smile. Another guy would be fantasizing about unwrapping said sari and exploring the woman underneath, but Billy wasn't like that. Oh, he was quite experienced. But now, older and wiser, he was holding out on her. How unfair was that?

"Maybe. Depends on where you have in mind. Bombay would be a little hard to get to. Where are you now?"

"The Universal lot," he reported. "Working on a set with Eduardo for the new Ron Howard movie. So we on for, say, seven?"

"Love to," Lydia agreed. Kat had mentioned something about taking Martina and Jimmy to visit friends down in Rancho Palos Verdes this evening, which meant Lydia might have a night of freedom. She and Billy hadn't spent much time together lately. For the last several weeks, he'd been up in the Bay Area, working on this same feature film. Called *Golden State,* it featured Jeff Bridges as a scientist hunting a mysterious creature that allegedly lived beneath the waters of San Francisco Bay.

Frankly, Lydia hadn't minded Billy's absence. Not because her feelings were cooling off, but because the whole Luis thing still niggled at her. Billy was such an honest guy. She knew her silence about Luis was deceitful. Now that she'd returned Luis's car and they'd had that talk on his doorstep, she and Billy could—and definitely should—move full steam ahead. In fact, the sooner she could get Billy undressed and doing what she'd wanted him to do, but which he supposedly wouldn't do, the better.

Lydia turned away from Martina and kept her voice low. "Oh, Billy."

"Oh, what?"

"You might get lucky tonight. Hint-hint."

Billy laughed. "Maybe I'll take that hint. But only if you can spend the night. Because I will need time."

What? Had he changed his mind about doing the deed with her? Her skin felt all tingly.

"Time?"

"Absolutely. What I plan cannot be rushed."

Oh yeah. As they said their goodbyes, she decided she definitely would be asking her aunt for the night off.

"Who was that?" Martina demanded.

"A friend."

"Who?"

Lydia scrunched her forehead. "You want me to give you some space with this guy Kevin? You give me some space with my friends. Fair's fair. Okay?"

Martina looked embarrassed. "Okay. I'm sorry."

Instantly, Lydia felt a little ashamed. "Look, I don't mean to be harsh. Want me to get you out of tennis?"

"How?" Martina challenged.

"Maybe we can wrap your ankle in an ACE bandage and say you sprained it doing jumping jacks for warm-up."

"Won't work. Momma Anya will check when we see her at the country club."

"Well, it'll get better fast," Lydia decided. "I'll say you wanted to do your tennis lesson but I insisted that you skip it, just to be on the safe side. You'll be totally off the hook."

"Really?"

"Really." Lydia was proud of herself for coming up with such an excellent fib. It really was an art form. "Then you can do whatever you want until it's time for lunch."

"Forget lunch. I'm not eating lunch." Martina looped some stringy hair behind her ear.

"I know the food sucks," Lydia acknowledged. "Back in Amazonia, no one would even feed it to their pigs. But I don't think we can get around mealtime. Paisley's in there, and you know how she watches every bite you eat. How about if I sneak you a bag of chips to go with it?"

"I meant I'm not eating lunch at all," Martina clarified. "I just decided."

Lydia sat back down on the edge of the bed. "Why not?"

Martina nibbled another ragged cuticle. "That was your boyfriend who just called, right?"

"Right."

Martina nodded. "He wouldn't like you if you were a big lump like me."

Oh Lord. Lydia patted the bed next to her. Martina sat. Lydia put an arm around her.

"First of all, you are not a 'lump.' You just need a chance to grow into your beauty. Second of all, my boyfriend would like me no matter what I looked like."

Lydia doubted very much if this was actually true, but knew this was another lie told for an excellent cause. American standards of beauty might be very different from Ama standards of beauty, but they were equally specific. Even a boy of Billy's fine character couldn't will himself to be attracted to a girl because she was beautiful on the inside.

Hot was hot. Not was not. Yet there was no need to impart that lesson to a girl about to enter the fifth grade.

Martina folded her arms. "You're lying."

Busted. Even a ten-year-old knew the truth, especially a ten-year-old in Beverly Hills.

"That's true. But you have to eat, sweet pea," Lydia insisted.

"No, I don't." Martina went to the wall calendar that hung next to her pink bulletin board. She put her finger on August twenty-fifth. "That's when school starts, in four weeks," she reported. "I have to lose fifteen pounds by then. I've made up all these excuses why I can't send Kevin a picture. But on the first day of school, he'll know the truth. For sure."

"If you exercise—" Lydia began.

"I've been exercising," Martina insisted. "I can do dumb-bell curls with fifteen pounds, but I'm not any skinnier." She sagged back against her pink pillows. "I lied to Kevin Covington. About what I look like."

"I know."

"Here. Look at him!" Martina went back to the computer and pushed a few keys. A photo of a spectacularly handsome boy filled the screen. He had long dark hair and dimples—a boy whom fifth-grade girls would swoon over. "His friends call him KC. Isn't that cool?" she added dreamily.

"He's very cute."

"He won't like me fat."

"You're not fat," Lydia insisted. "Besides, you can't not eat just because you want a boy to think you're cute."

"Why not? Half of Hollywood does. And I want to bleach my hair and get those colored contact lens thingies so that my eyes are green instead of blue."

"Martina, Momma Anya and Momma Kat are not going to let you bleach your hair or get contacts, sweetie. You're ten."

"I don't want to be the stupid, ugly fat girl anymore."

"You're not—"

"I am fat and ugly. Momma Anya thinks so! You said you're on my side. If you mean it, you'll help me. If not, then . . . then I'll tell Momma Anya all the stuff you've tried to do with me that's against the rules and they'll fire you."

Lydia's jaw fell open. Had her little cousin just threatened her?

"Martina, sweetie—"

"Not listening! Not listening!" Martina put her hands over her ears. "And I'm not eating, either. And there's nothing you can do to make me!"

8

Under a crystal blue noonday sky, Kiley and Susan—
Platinum's older sister—were lying out together on the pool
deck at the Brentwood Hills Country Club. Susan's husband,
Richard, was out on the golf course in a foursome, consisting
of Anya Kuriakova, a well-known Czech cinematographer, and
the manager of the Los Angeles Dodgers (who loved to play
the country club course on his off days).

Kiley was enjoying a moment of relative freedom, since Sid
and Serenity had gone to the restaurant for a burger—the
colonel heartily approved of red meat for growing children.
She wore the more-than-modest blue racing swimsuit purchased for her by *Platinum Nanny*.

She glanced over at Susan, who was rubbing SPF 50 sunblock into her white, freckled legs. If anything, Susan's swimsuit was even more modest than her own, and the opposite of

anything Susan's rock star sister would wear. It was kelly green with yellow piping around the boy-cut legs and neckline.

Save for her excellent cheekbones and azure blue eyes, it was hard to believe that Susan had any genetic relationship to Platinum. Her chin-length blond hair was styled in a flip that Kiley suspected not even gale-force winds could budge. This style never varied, except for various color-coordinated headbands or bows that often matched her kneesocks. Yes, the woman often wore kneesocks.

Kiley raised herself up on one elbow. It was the perfect opportunity to ask a question she'd wondered about since Susan and her husband had arrived at Platinum's estate to take charge of the children.

"Mrs. Jones?"

Susan put the sunblock back into her green and yellow straw tote bag and smiled. "If my husband isn't around, you can call me Susan, okay?"

"Okay. Susan." Kiley hesitated. "It's just that the colonel can be a bit . . ."

"Intimidating? Commanding? Overbearing?"

"Something like that," Kiley agreed.

"Did you ever see *The Great Santini*?"

Kiley shook her head. "What is it?"

"A movie. From a long time ago," Susan acknowledged. "The seventies. See if we can get it from Netflix. It'll tell you a lot about him." She dug a pair of yellow-rimmed sunglasses out of her bag and slipped them on. "When you take away all that marines stuff, you'll find an amazing man. I've never met anyone smarter. Or more loyal to his kids. To me. Or more

73

loving, in his own way. Of course, Rhonda hated him from the first time they met."

"Rhon—oh, you mean Platinum." Kiley laughed. She still couldn't get used to how Susan called Platinum by her given name instead of the stage name that the whole world used. As hard as she tried, imagining Platinum as a Rhonda was a stretch. On the other hand, Susan had just given Kiley the perfect opening to ask the question she'd been dying to ask. "If you wouldn't mind telling me . . . you and your younger sister are so different from each other. I was just wondering . . ."

"What happened?" Susan prompted.

Kiley nodded. As Susan tapped a contemplative short-nailed, polish-free finger against her lips, Kiley watched a girl from a MTV reality show stroll by in a bikini approximately the size of three postage stamps. Kiley knew that one of the strict country club regulations was that no photographs could be taken, which meant that guests didn't have to worry about whether paparazzi—professional or amateur—would be recording their bad hair days and/or inebriation at the nineteenth hole for posterity or a scandal sheet. The girl joined a cute guy in surfer Jams covered by a marijuana leaf pattern. Clearly wanting as much attention as possible, she squealed loudly as the boy tickled her. Then they locked lips. And pretty much everything else.

"Well . . . was Platinum like that when she was a teenager?" Kiley asked.

"Like what?" Susan asked.

"Like that girl over there," Kiley explained. "A show-off."

"Not exactly. First off, Rhonda is two years older than I am."

"*Older*?" Kiley couldn't believe it. "But all the bios I read—"

"I know." Susan shrugged. "Her PR people are really good at rewriting history, and the press is really good about repeating the rewrites. I know it's hard to believe."

True. Platinum looked a good decade younger than Susan. It was amazing what good hair, makeup, skin care, and Dr. Barry Weintraub's skills as a plastic surgeon could do.

"Anyway," Susan continued, "we were both born in Michigan, but after that we moved around a lot, and ended up in San Francisco in the seventies. We went to Catholic school there. I loved it but Rhonda hated it. She cut all the time and got into punk, which was just starting to be big. She was friends with Jello Biafra, Rocky Graham from the Symptoms, the guys from Eye Protection, the Mutants, the deejays at KSAN and then at KUSF—"

"How can you even remember all that?" Kiley asked.

Susan grinned conspiratorially. "I was the little sister. I knew them all, too."

Whoa. There was a whole hidden side to the colonel's wife that Kiley never could have imagined. "So they were your friends?"

"Not really. But they fascinated me. Rhonda brought them home sometimes. Even I wanted to be friends with them. . . . Well, I guess I just don't have the rebel gene. I was just a lot more studious than Rhonda. And religious. I worshipped the nuns. She worshipped the hardest of hard-core punk. Of course, we were just teens then. That was before she became a rock star in the eighties."

"So she started singing and you—?"

"Went to college in San Diego. To the University of San Diego. It's a Jesuit school—perfect for me." She drew her pale

75

knees up to her chest. "That wasn't my dream, though. What I really wanted to do was go to Scripps."

No way. Impossible.

"Did you say . . . Scripps?" Kiley queried. "The oceanography institute?"

Susan nodded. "It's in La Jolla—"

Kiley sat up. "That's where I want to go! That's why I auditioned for your sister's TV show—so I could establish California state residency and get in-state tuition. If I get in, of course. This is just so amazing!"

Susan smiled. "I wanted to work with dolphins. How about you?"

"I don't know yet," Kiley admitted. "There's just something about the ocean . . . I can't explain it. Why didn't you go to Scripps?"

"I didn't get in."

Kiley felt a physical pang, as if the rejection was happening to her. "That must have been so hard."

Susan nodded. "I was devastated. Anyway, I ended up studying elementary education instead."

Kiley couldn't get over it. What were the odds that she and Susan would have Scripps in common?

"So, go on," she urged, liking Susan more by the minute. "How did you meet the colonel?"

"At a church function." She looked into the distance, her eyes dreamy. "He was so responsible—an actual marine at Camp Pendleton and a practicing Catholic like me. I knew I could always depend on Richard." Her gaze went back to Kiley. "So, that's it. We got married, had our children, and I became a marine wife. Not something I necessarily recommend—hold on." She cocked her chin toward the far end of the pool deck, where the colonel and Anya, still dressed for golf, were approaching, laughing together about something. "I'll tell you more later," she added quickly.

"I'd like that."

A moment or two later, the colonel and Anya joined Kiley and Susan, unslinging their golf bags and plopping heavily down on two deck chairs.

"How did you play, dear?" Susan asked, reverting instantly to marine-wife mold.

"Like Tiger Woods!" the colonel boomed. He was tall and thin, with the perfect posture of a career military man, close-cropped gray hair, and a chiseled chin. He wore bright blue golf pants with a knife pleat and a white golf shirt with the Marine Corps logo emblazoned on the left chest.

"Like Tiger Woods on bad day with blindfold!" Anya hooted in her Russian accent.

To Kiley's shock, the colonel laughed heartily at Anya's dis.

"I shot an eighty-five," he admitted.

"And me eighty-three," Anya added proudly. "I beat him. Lucky for him we were not playing streep poker!"

"The actress?" the colonel joshed. "Meryl Streep poker?"

"Very funny joke!" Anya slapped him on the back and grinned broadly.

"You're a card, Anya," said the colonel. "Streep poker? A card? Get it?"

Anya roared with laughter. "A card? Like joker? You very funny man!"

Kiley stared at them in amazement. Not only was it the first time she'd ever seen Lydia's dour employer laugh, but it was also the first time she'd ever heard the colonel make anything approaching a joke.

He looked at his wife. "We're going to go get a beer. Susan, can you join us? Kiley, where are the children?"

"You should see them in the restaurant. They went in for a hamburger about fifteen minutes ago."

The colonel smiled, and winked at Anya. "Very good. If they're eating contraband, it's seven years in the stockade for them."

Anya roared with laughter again. Kiley looked at Susan, who wore a stiff smile as she slid off the chaise lounge and put on a terry cloth cover-up.

Anya clasped her hands together. "As your past president once said to our past president, *'Doveryay, no proveryay.'* "

"Trust, but verify!" the colonel translated.

Anya clapped him on the back again. "You are smart man." She turned to Kiley. "If you see Kat—she is on putting green— you tell where we are."

"Those are orders, McCann," the colonel barked.

"Yes, sir." Kiley had learned the hard way about not responding directly when the colonel asked her something.

Anya laughed again, and the two golfers headed off toward the restaurant-and-bar complex, with Susan bringing up the rear. Kiley was appalled. Never, ever would she marry a guy who treated her the way the colonel treated Susan. Never, ever, *ever*.

9

"You can hang out right over there." Jonathan pointed to a bank of monitors under a canopy that was set up in the parking lot of the rustic-looking convenience store in Topanga Canyon.

It was the very first day of production on *Montgomery*. The cast and crew would be at this convenience store, and the log cabin home located behind it, for the next week. Though still nominally inside the boundaries of Los Angeles, the convenience store and surrounding area had the look of small-town Alabama, where *Montgomery* (named for the main character, not the city) was set.

"You're sure it's okay?" Esme eyed the monitors and the handful of people sitting on black canvas director's chairs in front of them. They were laughing and chatting with one another; obviously at ease, which was definitely not how she felt on the walk down the hill from the movie's "base camp," where the cast and crew parked, equipment was stored, and the stars had their dressing trailers.

"Absolutely. They'll give you headphones, so you can watch and listen."

Esme felt fortunate to be able to visit the set on this weekday morning. Steven Goldhagen was working and Diane had taken the twins to a birthday party at the Museum of Television & Radio on North Beverly Drive. The birthday boy, Romeo, was the son of an actor-turned-director and a mother well known for her role on a long-running sitcom as the ditzy one in a group of longtime friends. The parents had decided to throw their child a "Make Your Own Sitcom" birthday party. Adult actors would be on hand with a professionally written script, and the kids would improvise around those scripts. The whole thing would be filmed and duplicated by a professional camera crew. Each kid would receive a copy of *Oh, Romeo!* once the editors finished cutting and splicing it.

According to Diane, the space at the museum in which they would be shooting was very small, so the invitation had asked that nannies not attend. Tarshea had volunteered to stay at the Goldhagens' and await the girls' arrival and subsequent nap. Diane had no objection. Esme was grateful. Having Tarshea around was proving to be incredibly helpful.

The night before, Esme had been so excited about Jonathan's invitation to the movie set. Everyone in Los Angeles was used to seeing movies made from afar. Traffic jams often resulted when word spread over www.gawkerholly wood.com, a Web site that posted who was spotted where.

She'd spent a good hour trying to figure out what to wear. She didn't want to look as if she was trying too hard. On the other hand, there were gorgeous girls in this movie with Jonathan. Since she'd be there as his girlfriend, she wanted to look hot. Finally she'd settled on tight black capris and a burnt orange Betsey Johnson camisole. Instead of a Valley girl high-heels-with-capris-means-I'm-trash look, she'd opted for black flats from an Echo shoe store where everything was under ten bucks, and hoped that their simplicity would keep people from realizing how cheap they were.

As she eyed the group of producers under the canopy, she felt nervous and insecure. "I might be in the way," she pointed out with as much sauciness as she could muster.

"Nah, it's fine," Jonathan assured her. "Just don't sit in any of the chairs that are marked Producer or Director." He kissed her lightly. "Gotta go. Time for my shot."

He headed toward the convenience store, having already explained that the upcoming sequence would be him coming out of the store and running into Mischa Barton, who played a high school sweetheart he'd dumped at prom two years before due to a misunderstanding. There were three cameras already aimed at the store, plus a burly guy testing a boom mike.

Esme took a deep breath. *Okay, you can do this,* she told herself.

Head held high, she strode into the canopied area. Immediately, a gorgeous young woman with red hair tumbling down her back stormed in after her. She carried a clipboard; her wireless headset was nearly obscured by her mass of curly hair.

"You." She pointed to Esme, who hoped there wasn't already a problem.

"Yes?"

"Laszlo is out of diet Mountain Dew."

Esme blinked. "Pardon?"

"I can't find Manuel—he always keeps Laszlo's cooler stocked, but I guess he's setting up for lunch. Go back to base camp and get him a cold six-pack. Now."

She thinks I'm the hired help.

"I'm Jonathan Goldhagen's girlfriend," Esme said stiffly.

"What? You're not with Craft Services?"

Esme shook her head.

"Sorry." The girl's face turned as red as her hair. "I'm Laszlo's second assistant, Daphne."

"Esme," she replied tersely.

Daphne backed away. "I'm so sorry. Really." She turned and scurried back toward the convenience store.

"Hey, Esme? Sit over here if you want," a slender, attractive blonde who looked to be in her forties suggested, and patted the chair next to hers. "It's Laszlo's, but he never sits with us. He has his own clamshell monitor that he carries with him."

"If you're sure it's okay . . ."

"It's fine," the woman assured her, and Esme slid into the seat. "I'm Sara Risher, one of the executive producers." She quickly introduced the other producers and assistants under the canopy. "Ever been on a movie set before?"

"No."

"It seems much more glamorous than it really is. Mostly it's a lot of hurry up and wait. They've been setting up this shot for the past hour. Then they'll shoot for ten minutes and go on to the next sequence. If they do three pages of script a day, that's pretty decent."

An African American girl with dreads, her headphone dangling off two fingers, eyed Esme with curiosity. Sara had introduced her as Vanya, a makeup artist. "So you snagged Jonathan Goldhagen, huh?"

Esme bristled. "I didn't snag anyone."

"Oh, girl, it's just a figure of speech, don't get all bent out of shape." Vanya waved a dismissive hand that held glittery rings on every finger, and a dozen bangle bracelets just below it. "I meant it as a compliment. I worked on *Tiger Eyes* when he was with that witch Mackenzie. I'm glad to see that the boy's taste has improved. Of course, it couldn't get much worse."

Esme laughed. "Thank you. I think."

"Vanya is notoriously outspoken," Sara quipped.

"Yet I keep getting hired anyway," Vanya pointed out. "So I must be damn good."

Daphne hustled back to them—it seemed to Esme that she was doing everything to avoid eye contact with her. "Bad news. Laszlo doesn't like the light. So we're breaking for lunch and we'll pick it up later."

"That puts us behind schedule. We'll never make our day!" Sara protested. "Where am I supposed to find the money to pay for overtime?"

Daphne shrugged. Meanwhile, everyone under the canopy took off their wireless headphones and placed them in the oversized canvas pockets attached to the arms of their chairs for just that purpose.

"And so it goes in the magical world of moviemaking." Sara sighed. "I'll show you the way to where we eat. You can meet Jonathan up there. Like I said, it's a lot of hurry up and wait."

Craft Services was serving lunch in a converted warehouse a half mile up the hill from the movie set. It was a massive operation, as the entire cast and crew lined up at three catering trucks to order tacos, fajitas, grilled and marinated Mexican steaks, and rice and red beans. Inside the warehouse were not only enough long tables and chairs to seat all hundred and fifty people comfortably, but also an extensive secondary buffet offering Caesar, spinach, fruit, and pasta salads; various breads, rolls, cheeses, and cold cuts; and a choice of desserts.

The atmosphere was noisy and convivial. After Jonathan had shepherded her through the buffet lines, she sat with him and the two actors who played his best friends, Tom Banachek and Preston Sheppard. The three actors were chuckling about something that had happened during the first shot of the day at the crack of dawn. Preston had sneezed violently in the middle of a take, and snot had flown out of his nose directly at the forty-something actress who played Jonathan's mother, Beverly Baylor. The booger had landed on Beverly's massive, silicone-enhanced cleavage. Obviously, Laszlo had called, "Cut!"

As they laughed, Esme took a bite of rice and washed it down with a glass of fresh lemonade. The food was delicious. Even better was how her boyfriend-the-actor periodically rubbed her back or let his hand wander under the table.

She knew she should feel great. Instead, she felt incredibly awkward and out of place. Jonathan said that the actors often had friends or family on the set, but she felt like she was the only outsider. It was just one step up from groupie.

"John-John!" a female voice purred. Beverly Baylor, whom Esme vaguely recognized from a soap opera her mother sometimes watched, stepped up behind Jonathan and leaned forward, breasts spilling out of her low-cut T-shirt. With it, she wore skinny black jeans and fuzzy pink slippers. "Are you being a bad boy and laughing about the snot shot with your friends?"

"Can you blame me?" Jonathan introduced Esme as his girlfriend, but Beverly barely glanced at her. Instead she edged forward and plopped herself in Jonathan's lap, helping herself with two dainty fingers to a cookie on his plate.

"I'll find a way for you boys to make it up to me." She looked at Esme and grinned coyly. "This doesn't mean anything."

"I don't own his lap." As soon as the words were out of her mouth, Esme regretted them. What a bitchy thing to say to someone you'd never met before.

Beverly licked a crumb from her index fingertip. "But as Jonathan's girlfriend, you should claim squatter's rights. If you don't, your loss." Her attention fell on Jonathan's arm. He'd taken off the long-sleeved denim shirt that was part of his costume, and his tattoo was now visible, the Ferris wheel still covered in protective plastic coating. "Wow. That is awesome. I've never seen anything like it."

"Yeah? Esme did it."

Beverly's eyebrows rose. "Who did the stencil? Esme, can you get me one?"

"No stencil," Esme reported. "I did it freehand."

Tom leaned over the table and stared at the tattoo. "No freaking way you did that freehand."

Jonathan grinned. "Yes freaking way. She's an artist."

Beverly hopped off Jonathan's lap and lifted the very bottom of her T-shirt. There was a tattoo of Chinese lettering in that oh-so-popular small-of-the-back region where Esme refused on principle to do tattoos. How boring.

"See this? The tattoo guy in Vegas told me it said *peaceful soul*. Then my herbalist from Beijing tells me it really says *dead possum*. Can you believe it?"

Esme bit her lip to keep from cracking up. That was what the stupid woman got for trusting a tattoo artist she didn't know.

"Anyway, I'm getting it lasered off when I wrap my shoot here. Esme, you have to do a new one for me."

Esme was taken aback. "I don't—I mean—I usually only do friends."

And gang members back in the Echo.

Beverly flung her arms wide and embraced her in a bear hug. "Friend! Now, let's get down to business. What do you charge?"

"Three-fifty a tattoo or two hundred an hour," Jonathan volunteered, before Esme could formulate a response. "Whichever is higher."

"Sweet," Tom crowed as Beverly nodded her acquiescence to the quoted fee. "Hey, there's this spot in Maui—best place on earth, man. It's where I met my wife. You think if I showed you a photograph you could ink it into my upper back? What's your estimate on time for something like that, Esme? Three hours? Four?"

"Four," Esme managed to choke out. She was doing math in her head, and the amount of money that was coming up was more than she could have dreamed.

"No sweat," Tom assured her. "For that kind of craftsmanship, I'm in."

Beverly shoved a small, stapled set of papers at Esme. It was a miniature version of her script for the next scene. "Jonathan, give your girlfriend a pen. Esme, put your name and phone number here on the back and I'll call you to arrange everything. Can you do it at my place in Santa Monica? As soon as possible?"

Esme hesitated. This was all happening much too fast. The only people besides Jonathan whom she had tattooed were gang members. Wouldn't these actors just shit if they knew that? Actually, they'd probably think it was cool.

What the hell. She scribbled her name and her cell number and added "tattoos" after it. Suddenly, the idea of getting paid massive amounts of money to inject these people with painful decorative ink was very appealing indeed.

10

Lydia and Martina walked past the putting green, the bunker practice area, and the pro shop on their way to the Brentwood Hills Country Club driving range, where Jimmy was taking his very first golf lesson. As they made their way, Lydia eyed her not-so-little cousin with concern. Since Martina's declaration the day before that she was going on a hunger strike, she hadn't eaten anything at all. Neither of the moms was aware of this new regime, since they hadn't been present at mealtimes and Jimmy was keeping his mouth shut. But it couldn't stay a secret forever. Lydia had pretty much decided that if she couldn't get her cousin to see the foolishness of her decision by the end of the day, she'd be forced to turn Martina over to the moms squad.

Lord knows what Anya will do, Lydia thought. *Force-feed the kid bean sprouts or something.*

"Hey, I've got a great idea. After we meet Jimmy, want to go to the restaurant? For a bacon double cheeseburger with lots of mayo and broiled onions?" Lydia offered. "You know how much you love them."

Martina cut her eyes at Lydia. "N-O. No."

"How about a piece of that famous Brentwood Hills Country Club chocolate cheesecake and a scoop of homemade butter pecan ice cream? Or a chocolate milk shake?"

Martina put her hands on her hips, or at least where her hips would have been if she hadn't been camouflaged in a three-sizes-too-large red sweatshirt and khaki pants. Lydia knew the girl had to be dying in those clothes, because it was a swelteringly hot day for Los Angeles. Lydia herself wore Ralph Lauren baggy white shorts held up with an orange silk necktie she'd found for a buck at a vintage store in the Valley, and a yellow bra top from a Chloé bikini under a sheer Marc Jacobs orange and pink polka-dot peasant shirt. It wasn't much, but it was much more than what she'd wear in Amazonia on days like these. Her fading allover tan could attest to that.

"Whose side are you on?" Martina demanded.

"Yours, sweet pea, you must know that by now. Which is why I want you to eat."

Resolute, Martina shook her head.

Lydia sighed. She could only imagine how painful it was to be a little girl in a big girl's very developed body. She vowed to think of some way to get Martina to eat. Anything was better than turning her over to Anya.

"Golf is stupid," Martina decreed as they watched people at the driving range swinging their clubs more or less successfully. Usually, less.

"It doesn't float my dugout, either," Lydia admitted.

She tried to imagine what her Ama friends and neighbors would think of the game. Not much, she decided, as she watched a couple of movie stars she recognized from the magazines she'd devoured in the jungle try to smack balls out of a sand trap. She was pretty sure he was the guy who had gotten famous in the first *Star Wars* movie and then become an action hero; his partner was equally well known for both playing a thirty-something lawyer in a TV show and for being so skinny that she was probably Martina's role model.

"Do they play golf in the Amazon?" Martina suddenly asked.

"Nope. Well, let me modify that. There is a game where you throw a severed monkey head in the air and then try to whack it with a stick—"

Martina put her hands in the vicinity of her stomach. "Eww! That's disgusting!"

"We always ate the rest," Lydia reasoned. "So why should the head go to waste? On the other hand, I can think of few tribesmen who wouldn't mind clubbing a wild boar to death with a five iron if they were out of blow darts."

"Did you ever use a blowgun?"

"Oh yeah, sure. All the time."

Martina pushed back her curtain of hair and peered at Lydia—sure signs that curiosity had momentarily won out over self-consciousness. "So . . . how does it work? A blowgun, I mean?"

"With a firing tube. And a dart. One that usually has poison on the tip."

"Shut *up*!" Martina exclaimed, wide-eyed. "Where do you get one?"

Lydia knew Martina did not really mean "shut up" but rather "oh, wow," and that Martina was only using the expression because the prettiest and most petite blond girl at Nanny and Me used the expression on a regular basis.

"Well, first you learn how to make your own gun and then you learn how to make the darts," Lydia explained. "It's not like you can run over to Wal-Mart and pick one up in the sporting goods department. You have to practice over and over before you get to where you even come close to hitting your target."

Martina nodded. "And they let girls do it, too?"

"Of course. The girls were better at it than the boys," Lydia added, which wasn't true in general but was true in her case. She had become the best shot in their little village, much to the chagrin of various seminaked young tribesmen. Lydia figured that when it came to insecure Martina, anything she could say or do that would play up the ability of girls was a good thing, lies for a good purpose included.

"So, like how old were the girls who were good at it?"

"Well, the elders wouldn't even think about letting kids start learning until they were ten."

Martina grabbed Lydia's arm. "I'm ten! Teach me."

This was not the response Lydia had expected. Martina rarely showed interest in learning anything.

"Well, um . . ."

"Come on. I'm old enough."

Lydia didn't like where this conversation was going, though

she had to admit there were plenty of times when she would have liked to plant a high-velocity curare-tipped projectile in Anya's well-toned ass.

Martina clutched Lydia's arm even harder. "Pretty please?"

"Why in the world do you want to learn about blowguns? They're weapons, not toys."

Martina kicked the heel of her sneaker into the short grass. "I know. It's just that . . . well, there's nothing really cool that I do that I can tell . . . oh, forget it. It's not important."

Oh. Of course. This was about Kevin, who'd been led to believe via e-mail that Martina was blond, skinny, and wildly popular. Well, she was right about one thing: no other fifth grader at the Crossroads School would try to impress him with her firsthand knowledge of how to use a blowgun.

"Fine. I'll teach you," Lydia declared.

Martina clasped her hands together. "Really?"

"*If.*"

Martina's shoulders sagged. "I should have known there was a catch. There's always a catch."

"It's because I'm clever and manipulative. Anyway, there are two catches. One: You end this danged hunger strike and we go to the restaurant and you order a meal. Two: Never—and I mean never, *ever*—shoot it unless I'm around."

"That's not fair!" Martina wailed.

"Now, see, if you go crying like a big ol' baby, that's just proof that you're not old enough."

"I am *not* a baby."

"And I am not changing any part of this deal. When I'm teaching you, you have to do exactly what I say when I say it, and if I ever catch you fooling around or not treating it like the weapon it is, I'll break it over my knee and present both pieces to Momma Anya with your name on them."

Martina paled. "She'd kill me."

"After she kills me. At least if I go first I wouldn't have to watch you die. So . . . deal or no deal?"

"I guess . . . deal."

"Shake on it." Lydia stuck out her hand. "Including the eating part."

Martina solemnly shook her hand as Lydia mentally congratulated herself on her own negotiating skills. Right after Jimmy finished his lesson she'd take the kids to the snack bar.

They spotted him a moment later on the driving range, with an oversized Big Bertha driver in his hands and three red-striped golf balls teed up on the ground. As soon as he noticed his sister and big cousin approaching, he grinned.

"Hey, check this out." He took a swing and hit the ball straight out to the two-hundred-yard marker, then did the same thing with the second ball. "Sweet, huh?"

"Good job!" Lydia was impressed.

"Aww, that's nothing. Check this out."

Jimmy took three running steps, charged up to the third ball, swung at it with all his might, and missed completely, falling so clumsily onto the grass that his club flew ten feet out onto the range. Twenty feet away down the range, Weston Goldhagen laughed so hard at the sight that she pointed at him and jumped up and down.

"Look Jee-mee! Jee-mee funny!"

"Jee-mee do like Happy Gilmore for Weston!" He pumped his fist in the air, making it clear that he was clowning around.

This was great. Neither of her young cousins had ever made

jokes when she'd first arrived from the Amazon. Lydia herself would have laughed at Jimmy's antics, except that she noted who was helping Weston with her swing: One-night-stand Luis.

He waved to Lydia. She waved back.

"He's cute, that golf teacher," Martina decided, shading her face from the sun with her hand. "Do you like him?"

"No," Lydia said. "I have a boyfriend, remember? Billy?"

Martina frowned. "Didn't you tell me that it was a good thing for a girl to have *lots* of boyfriends?"

"Uh-huh," Lydia admitted. "But sometimes if you really like one boy a whole, whole lot, you don't feel like being with any other boys."

"So, you like Billy a whole, whole lot?"

"Yep."

And I cheated on him with your brother's teacher.

Lydia watched as Luis set up a long-drive contest between Weston and Jimmy. Her own feelings galled her. Since when had she become so *conventional* about sex?

"Tee 'em up," Luis told the kids.

Instantly, Jimmy and Weston each teed up another golf ball and took their stances.

"One . . . two . . . three!" Luis counted off.

Two golf clubs arced back and then swung forward in perfect reverse parabolas. The kids spun their hips and made contact at the same time. Jimmy's ball went farther—out to the two-hundred-yard marker, as opposed to Weston's hundred-and-twenty-five-yard shot. Lydia was more impressed with Weston, though, since the girl was only six.

"Yes!" Jimmy pumped his fist. "Another perfect hit!"

Lydia stepped over to her cousin and hugged him. "Well, you just rock!" she crowed. "You like this sport?"

"So much," he told her.

"It was a great first lesson," Luis acknowledged, joining them. "I'm proud of you, Jimmy. I'll see you later in the week?"

"Definitely," Jimmy agreed. "Golf is a lot more fun than tennis, no lie. It's even better than bugs."

"C'mon, Jimmy," Martina cajoled. "I'm hungry. Let's go up to the restaurant. I want a burger. A jumbo bacon cheeseburger."

"You're eating again?" Jimmy was surprised.

"Yeah. Lydia told me she'd—she told me that it would be a good idea to eat. So I listened."

Martina shot a guilty look at Lydia, knowing that she'd almost spilled why she'd decided to end her hunger strike. Lydia merely shrugged. As they said in Amazonia: no cut, no blood, no piranha attack.

"Cool," Jimmy agreed. "Let's get something good if the moms aren't there."

Lydia nodded. "Go ahead, you guys. I'll catch up with you. Luis, I can take Weston up to the pool and wait for Esme."

"Great. I'm heading to the restaurant myself. I'll walk you up." He gave her a sexy grin. "I won't bite."

"Yes, he won't bite you," Weston repeated, which made Lydia laugh. The twins had learned so much English over the last several weeks that it was a little frightening. Of course, she'd learned the Ama language in the jungle, but that was a tongue with far fewer tenses and basically no adjectives.

Luis moved closer to Lydia so that only she could hear him. "Of course, if you *want* me to bite . . ."

Lydia wagged a friendly finger at him. "Come on, Luis. Remember that chat we had on your doorstep?"

"I thought it was a lady's prerogative to change her mind." His eyes flicked over her as if he knew what she looked like naked, which he most certainly did. "We had a good thing."

Fortunately, Weston was distracted by a red admiral butterfly as it flitted across the path.

"I don't know about you, Luis. But for me, one-time sex I don't remember that occurred under the influence of alcohol doesn't live on in my personal hall of flame."

"Hall of *flame*," Luis echoed. "Cute."

"Well honey, you just don't seem to be getting the big N-O tattooed on my forehead."

"Aww, come on, Lydia. I've got a pair of tickets burning a hole in my pocket. Skybox seats to the Dodgers—I gave the manager a lesson with his pitching wedge." As if to prove his point, he opened his black leather wallet and displayed the ducats. "Champagne in the fridge, comfortable couches . . . what could be bad?"

"Luis, I'm sure that lots of cute girls at this club would do anything to hook up with a cute golf pro. How about if I just send them your way?" Lydia said sweetly.

"How about if I trade them for you?" he joked.

Jeez. Luis was beginning to really annoy her. She hoped he got the message from the silent treatment she offered in response to his last question, all the way up to the family pool.

11

As Lydia and Luis made their silent journey up the hill from the driving range, Kiley sat with her feet dangling in the shallow end of the country club's family pool, watching Sid and Serenity play water basketball. The colonel's regime might be authoritarian, she thought, but there was no doubt that Platinum's kids were in better physical shape as a result of it. Before the arrival of the colonel and Susan, ten minutes of water basketball would have had them sucking wind. Now they'd become superstars, making passes and sinking shots that would have been impossible even three weeks ago.

Suddenly, a large pair of hands slipped over her eyes. "Guess who?"

There was only one voice in America like that. Her breath caught.

"Tom?"

She swung around, and there he was, crouching by the side

of the pool, grinning at her. His blond hair was shorter than the last time she'd seen him; his deep tan made his eyes look even bluer, his Chiclet white teeth even whiter. He wore red surfer Jams and nothing else. His ripped torso was hairless, tanned, and perfect. He looked exactly like what he was—a monumentally successful model.

"When did you get back?" Kiley cut her eyes back toward the country club restaurant. She didn't want the colonel to see her talking with Tom instead of doing her job.

"This morning." He sat next to her, playfully bumping his muscled thigh into hers. "How goes it?"

"Fine. But . . . I wish you had called me."

"I wanted to surprise you." He cocked his head at her. "That a bad thing?"

"No, it's just I'm working."

"So I see." Tom nodded toward the kids. Sid had just made a great dunk; his team cheered. Tom cheered with them. "Nice job, Sid!"

"How was Florida?"

"The usual modeling nonsense, but I banked a nice chunk o' change. Sent it to my dad so he could buy a new combine and pay off a bunch of debt. The corn harvest last fall was kinda shaky."

Kiley's heart melted at the mention of his parents' farm. She had so much in common with him. Half of her friends back in La Crosse had been in 4H or FFA. Could he help it that he was a farm boy who was ten standard deviations better-looking than average?

"That was a nice thing to do."

"It's my pops." Tom grinned. "But listen, if I ever decide to take over the family farm, please send me to a shrink. My dad works his butt off and no one appreciates it."

"You do."

"Yeah," Tom admitted. "I do." His fingers brushed the back of her hand. It gave her chills. "It's great to see you. I missed you. So did you fall in love while I was away?"

She'd never been a good liar, and always considered it one of her strong points. The moment Tom posed the question, she flashed to Jorge and the way he'd kissed her at the Conga Room. It must have registered on her face, because Tom frowned.

"Hey, that was supposed to be a joke."

She was taken aback by the stunned look in his eyes.

"Tom, it's just that . . ."

Out of the corner of her eye, she saw the colonel and Susan returning to the pool deck. "Look, I can't talk now. My boss is coming."

He scrambled to his feet. "To be continued."

"Call me later."

"Yeah, okay."

He rubbed his chin, seemingly puzzled and—was it really possible? Hurt.

Kiley slid into the pool, swimming over to the basketball game so that she could make a show of participating with the children. She'd just fired a pass to Sid when she heard the colonel call to her from the pool's edge.

"McCann!"

"Yes, sir?"

She resisted the urge to salute. Instead, she swam over to the nearest ladder and climbed out of the pool. He was waiting for her with a towel and a clipboard.

"Scuba!" he boomed. He offered her the towel. "What's your take on that, McCann?"

Kiley dried herself off, then wrapped the towel around her waist and tucked in the edge. "That it's self-contained under-water breathing apparatus, sir."

She wasn't about to add that she knew scuba diving was a requirement for any self-respecting marine biologist. Or that back in La Crosse, scuba diving had been a recreational activity only for those wealthy enough to go away on winter vacations to Hawaii and Jamaica. Since Kiley's winter vacations tended toward car trips to Appleton to see her aunt, she'd never learned.

"I want you to learn, McCann. Right here at the club." He thrust the clipboard at her. "This is the registration form. Classes begin day after tomorrow. I've already paid the fees. Sign at the X."

Kiley took the outstretched pen before the colonel could change his mind, thinking that Susan might have talked to him about her interest in Scripps. "This is fantastic! I've wanted to learn to scuba dive forever."

"The missus mentioned your aquatic interests," the colonel barked. "This will be a good opportunity for you. Bruce too."

"Bruce?"

"Yes, McCann. He's going to be joining you."

Huh. Good luck. Thus far, the colonel's attempts to shape up Platinum's fourteen-year-old had been met with nonviolent civil disobedience worthy of Mahatma Gandhi. As a result, he'd been confined to quarters—his bedroom—every night for the past two weeks, and had done more push-ups than a linebacker at summer training camp. Now the colonel wanted Bruce to learn to scuba dive?

"Sir?"

"McCann?"

"Permission to speak freely, sir."

The colonel put his hands behind his back. "Permission granted, McCann. What's on your mind?"

"Sir, I doubt that Bruce is going to want to learn to—"

"Stop right there, McCann," the colonel interrupted. "*Want* doesn't cut it with me. This is not a matter of what he wants. This is a matter of what he needs. Are we clear on that?"

"Yes, sir," Kiley replied, still highly dubious. "I hope you can convince him, sir."

The colonel laughed. "That's the second part of your assignment, McCann. I wish you all the luck in the world."

12

The white-jacketed Indian waiter was about to take the lid off one of the crockery dishes when Billy stopped him. "Wait a second, Kumar. I want to give her the full experience. Close your eyes." Billy grinned across the small table at Lydia.

"Billy Martin. If you think you're going to shock me by having me close my eyes and then making me eat something nasty, you have got the wrong girl." Lydia didn't know why it was that whenever she was with him, her Texas drawl got more pronounced. It was as if she allowed her own authentic self to surface for him. "I have eaten roasted mealworm and fried monkey guts. How about you?"

Kumar paled.

"Interesting girl," Billy told the waiter, then gazed again at Lydia with his deep blue eyes. "You'll have to trust me."

"Billy. My parents homeschooled me in a mud hut. Nothing makes you learn quicker than red ants biting your butt."

Billy laughed. "You, Lydia Chandler, are one of a kind. Okay, Kumar. Lid off the vegetable biryani. Lydia, close 'em."

"Since when did you get so bossy?"

She closed her eyes in happy anticipation. It wasn't for the Indian food, much as Billy had rhapsodized about how this particular restaurant across from the Westside Pavilion in the Rancho Park section of the city was the best in all of Los Angeles. Mostly, she was imagining him in bed with her, doing what came naturally. She'd enjoyed the look in his eyes when he'd picked her up and saw what she was wearing—a L.A.M.B. by Gwen Stefani leopard-print minishift with a flirty short-sleeved white lace blouse underneath, and purple studded Marc Jacobs ankle boots with a three-inch heel that her aunt Kat had given to her outright.

What Billy didn't know was that under the lace blouse and minishift, Lydia wore nothing else. No bra, no thong, nothing. All the better for dessert.

The restaurant was called Jaipur, and it turned out that Kumar was the son of the owner. Evidently, Billy ate here a lot. Kumar had led them through the dark-walled interior to a table in the back, not far from the to-go counter. With ragas playing on the sound system, Indian artwork on the walls, and unfamiliar but mouthwatering aromas wafting out of the kitchen, Lydia felt like she could be half a world away.

"Okay," Billy said. "Taste this."

Lydia opened her mouth. The motion made her think of sex. Tonight, everything was making her think of sex.

"It's hot," he warned.

Lydia nearly laughed out loud. Maybe he was on her wavelength, too. A delicious mix of aromas wafted into her

103

nostrils—saffron, cream, curry, pepper, onions, maybe eggplant, something sweet but not sugary. Then the fork was in her mouth, and smells turned into a panoply of amazing flavors unlike anything she'd ever tasted.

She chewed with gusto, swallowed, and then opened her eyes as languidly as possible. "That's amazing. What was that?"

"Began bharta—specialty of the house," Kumar said proudly. "I'm glad you like it."

"I love it!" Lydia exclaimed.

"It's eggplant baked in a tandoori oven, special red onions, ginger imported from Mumbai, hothouse yellow tomatoes, and some other spices," Billy filled in. Kumar gave a little bow and said he would leave them to enjoy their meal. When he was gone, Lydia stuck her own fork into the clay pot.

"I think we should move in here," she declared, forking up another mouthful of the delicious concoction. "Or maybe Kumar could sleep in your living room and cook for us. Three meals a day, I don't demand much." She spooned some of the food onto Billy's plate, then filled her own.

Billy cocked an eyebrow. "How would that work, since you don't live in my apartment?"

"Just think how much fun we could have if I did," she flirted.

"On a nightly basis," he added.

She reached across the table and entwined her fingers with his large, strong ones. "I have a secret, Billy. Something I really need to tell you. I should have told you before, but . . ."

She hesitated. He put his fork down. "Okay."

She leaned in to him. "I'm not wearing any underwear."

He burst out laughing. "Aren't you the naughty girl."

"Not yet," she reminded him. "But I'd like to be. After we finish this amazing food, that is."

Billy gave her a smoldering look. "Tonight's the night, huh?"

"You wanted us to wait, we waited. You wanted us to get to really know each other, we know each other." Under the table she lifted one purple-booted foot and slid it along the leg of his jeans. "So yes. Tonight is the night. Even if I have to tie you down."

Billy licked some sauce from his pinky. "Or maybe I'll have to tie you down."

Well, this was going really, really well. At least he was saying the right things, which was a damn lot better than where he'd been on the issue before. It was a lot easier to get someone to say yes when that person was in the habit of saying yes. Very promising. Tonight she and Billy would seal the deal. And Luis would barely be a—

No. It couldn't be. Lydia peered toward the front of the restaurant, where someone who looked a lot like Luis was picking up a to-go order.

He turned. It *was* Luis. He was looking right at her.

Damn. Of all the shit-ass luck.

When Luis recognized her, he popped a pair of earbuds from his ears and walked confidently toward her and Billy's table. "Well, well. If it isn't the great Lydia Chandler? What a surprise. You've got good taste in restaurants."

"Actually, my boyfriend picked it," Lydia said, feeling incredibly uncomfortable to be in between these two guys in one room. She quickly introduced Billy to Luis, explaining that Luis was the country club pro who'd given Jimmy his first lesson.

The two guys shook hands. "Nice to meet you," Billy told him politely.

"You too," Luis agreed. "You play?"

"I surf a little and played soccer in high school. But no golf."

Lydia watched the two guys with trepidation. Surely Luis would have the good sense not to do or say anything to indicate that their relationship went beyond a country club acquaintanceship.

All he did was tell them to enjoy their meal.

"Sure," she agreed, keeping a cheerful look on her face and reminding herself that she owed Luis exactly nothing.

"Have a wonderful night. See you at the club sometime. Billy, you're a lucky guy. She's really something." A discreet bell sounded, and Luis headed back to the counter to pick up his to-go bags.

"Lydia's 'really something'?" Billy echoed.

"Oh, you know me, always joking around at the club," Lydia said lightly. "It helps relax Jimmy. He's such a tense kid, and he really wants to be good at golf."

Billy nodded and sipped his Kingfisher beer in its green can. Meanwhile, Lydia fumed. What was Luis doing making a comment like that?

She excused herself to go to the bathroom and caught up with Luis on the sidewalk outside the restaurant.

"I thought I could count on you," she told him. "To be discreet."

Luis laughed. "Hold on. All I did was come in for some takeout."

"Lydia's 'really something'? 'You're a lucky guy, Billy'? That's *takeout*?"

"You need to relax, Lydia," the golf pro told her. "I wasn't born yesterday. And now, I'm going home to eat this delicious food." He gave a little wave and headed toward his Spyder, parked right behind Billy's red Saab by the curb outside the restaurant.

It was almost as if he'd intentionally pulled into the spot right behind them.

"Luis!"

He looked up as he opened his front door.

"Tell me—did you follow me here, Luis?" Her clenched throat raised her words half an octave.

She didn't feel any better when Luis didn't answer. Instead, he shook his head ruefully, got into the car, and drove away.

13

Kiley knocked on Bruce's white-painted door, now stripped of the rock-and-roll posters that used to adorn it. Nothing. She knocked again, louder. Still nothing. She knew he was in there, though, because she'd been smart enough to put a piece of tape between the door and the jamb earlier. If Bruce had snuck out, the tape would have been torn. It wasn't.

"Come on, Bruce. It's me, Kiley. Don't be a pain in the—"

The door swung open. There stood Bruce, in a pair of jeans and an old Bruce Springsteen T-shirt. When Kiley had been preparing for the reality show, she'd come across rampant Internet rumors that this Bruce was the offspring of *that* Bruce. Now she was aware that Platinum herself had fueled the speculation for publicity purposes.

Once upon a time, back when the rock star had been the mistress of her own domain, Bruce's room would have approximated a federal disaster area. Now, in the colonel era, it looked like a plebe's quarters at West Point. Everything was neat, the bed perfectly made with hospital corners. There were no stray objects or even discarded clothing on the floor.

"Welcome to San Quentin," Bruce growled. "And if that asshole tells me to secure my bunk and police the area, he's getting Ex-Lax in his blood pressure meds."

"Why didn't you open for me when I knocked?"

"I thought you were him."

Kiley sympathized with Bruce. The colonel had turned the kids' world upside down and sideways with his overnight imposition of military discipline. Under the ancien régime, Bruce had been granted total autonomy and complete freedom. Not that total freedom was good for a fourteen-year-old, either.

"Are you confined to quarters?"

"Until next Wednesday. He didn't like the way I mowed the back lawn. I did it back and forth, he wanted it on the diagonal crisscrossed like the outfield at goddamn Dodger Stadium. We have three goddamn gardeners, why am I out there working?"

"Um . . . to learn discipline?" Kiley asked weakly.

"I hate that asshole." Bruce leaned against the doorframe. "What do you want?"

"Number one, I'd recommend you cut back on the swearing. It could get habit-forming, and the colonel won't be happy. Can I come in?" Kiley asked. Bruce moved out of the way with a petulant look on his face, but Kiley plunged ahead. "So, let's talk about getting you sprung."

For the first time, Bruce showed a modicum of interest. Kiley couldn't blame him. Here it was, seven o'clock on a Saturday night. Bruce was a party animal who had a lot of young friends who were as into music as he was. Because of Platinum's connections, they could always get great tickets to see whoever was in town. Kiley knew he was a huge Yellowcard fan. That band was playing this very evening at the Hollywood Bowl; Bruce was missing the show because he was confined to quarters. He couldn't even sneak out, since the colonel controlled the electronic gate at the bottom of the driveway and an impenetrable hedge surrounded the rest of the property.

Bruce kicked his door shut, then put a pair of combative hands on his hips. "Okay. Talk to me. What's your great idea to get me off death row?"

"The colonel is paying for me to take scuba lessons."

"Please. Take him along and fill his air tanks with ultra-long-lasting sleeping gas."

"I don't think that's possible. He wants you to learn, too."

Bruce snorted out a laugh. "That's a joke. He thinks because he wants me to do it, I'm going to do it? Believe me, I'll do the opposite of what he wants."

"That will only piss him off even more. Which would only result in even more time confined to quarters."

"Too bad. I'll never do what he wants. I don't want to give him the satisfaction." Bruce folded his arms and set his jaw.

Kiley expected this reaction.

"Fair enough. I was going to invite you and your friends to come along when my friends and I go diving at Catalina Island, but if you can't scuba—no point. I could make a really great case for the colonel to let you come with us. Too bad. It would be an all-day thing." She turned and headed for the door.

"Wait!"

Bingo.

Kiley looked over her shoulder. "Yeah?"

Bruce pursed his lips. "You really think that if I get certified the colonel will let me go on dives without him?"

She knew better than to bullshit him. "I think you've at least got a shot. He can't be in two places at once. If it was me in your shoes, I'd take my chances."

"Huh." He seemed to be considering his options. "When does class start?"

"Tomorrow, at the club. Adult pool. Eleven o'clock. You want a ride?"

"Let me think about it."

"You do that," she agreed.

"Just wondering . . ." He scratched the soul patch he was attempting to grow below his lower lip. "How cute are your friends?"

"Very. 'Night."

She walked out and closed his door behind her, hiding a proud smile. Maybe all this time in Los Angeles was turning her into a mistress of manipulation just like everyone else. If she was a betting girl she would have wagered the estate that Bruce would be in the pool with her tomorrow.

Not that she owned the estate. But still.

The colonel pushed his rook forward one space. "Check."

"Ah. You attack. This calls for more vodka, no?" Without waiting to see if her opponent agreed, Anya tilted the three-quarter-full Flagman bottle and poured two generous shots.

"Pour away. Vodka did not help your side in the cold war, it won't help it now," the colonel cracked.

"What do you know of cold war?" Anya asked.

"I was with the marines in the middle of it. At Camp Pendleton."

Anya twirled a pawn between her slender fingers. "So? My father was on B-4 class submarine during Cuban Missile Crisis, deployed off coast of California. He had missile aimed at your Camp Pendleton. Also San Diego, Long Beach, and Los Angeles where we sit. My dad one tough guy. You lucky to be here to play chess with me."

"Oh, really?" the colonel retorted. "Last time I looked, the United States of America was still the United States of America, and the Soviet Union was consigned to the dustbin of history."

"Civilizations rise, civilizations fall. *Na zdorov'ya*. To your good health. And to rise of new Russia." She clinked her glass with his, downed the vodka in one big shot, and then moved a bishop to block the assault by the colonel's rook. "Is no more check for you. Is same bad move made by Big Blue against Garry Kasparov. Is now check for me. Good luck, Colonel, you will need."

Kiley stood at the bottom of the stairs—she'd been heading down to the kitchen to get something to eat, but the sight of the colonel and Anya hunched over the chessboard with a vodka bottle between them had stopped her dead in her tracks. The chessboard they played on was magnificent, built right into a white marble coffee table, with large classic ivory pieces and two small wells for captured chessmen. The colonel and Anya sat on matching upholstered eggshell velvet chairs with intricate carvings between the legs. Rays of late evening sun shone through the west-facing windows. She realized that since the colonel and Susan had arrived at Platinum's household, this was the first time there had been any social visitors at all.

Anya and the colonel were not just golf rivals?

She cleared her throat.

"Good evening, McCann." The colonel offered his usual greeting.

"Good evening, Colonel."

"Hello, Kiley," Anya told her. "I defeat colonel on the golf course, he offered me return match on chessboard. Of course I accept. Nothing more fun than to defeat American opponent. He is on verge of humiliation. Is good, no?"

Oh. Now it all made sense. Anya had met someone as competitive as she was.

"I was on the way to the kitchen," Kiley explained. "Colonel, is there anything you'd like me to do tonight with Sid or Serenity?"

"I don't think so, McCann. How'd it go with Bruce?"

"I think I've convinced him, sir."

The colonel beamed. "Excellent, McCann. Outstanding. I knew you had it in you. Why don't you take the evening off?"

The colonel had just offered her a night off, without prompting? Usually, Kiley had to clear her free evenings forty-eight hours in advance.

"What about Sid and Serenity?" Kiley knew better than to look a gift evening in the mouth, but maybe the colonel would take notice and cut her some future slack for being responsible.

"Fear not, McCann. The missus took them to visit her ding-a-ling sister, supervised by Ms. Johnson. Dinner at Mel's

Drive-in." The colonel named a small chain of low-priced fifties-style Los Angeles diners famous for serving their kids' meals in cardboard cars.

"Mel's Drive-in is poison. Additives, grease! This is not food for children!" Anya was incensed.

"Affirmative. But the kids picked it and the social worker approved it. Whose move is it?"

"Is your move, Colonel."

"Thank you, Anya. McCann, what are you standing there for? Do you need an invitation? I just granted you liberty for the night." He winked at Anya. "Now skedaddle before I change my mind."

Kiley was in a state of shock. The colonel was grinning, and Anya was giggling like a fourth grader who'd just heard a mildly dirty joke.

"Thanks. Sir," she added hastily.

Kiley passed through the living room to the kitchen as inconspicuously as possible, stopping only to snare a ripe Bartlett pear from the fruit bowl on the round bleached blond wooden table before heading outside to the Lotus. An intoxicating evening of freedom awaited her. Whom should she call?

"And the sex was amazing," Lydia concluded, dropping a giant picnic basket onto an oversized rattan ground covering that she'd just spread carefully on the grass outside the Hollywood Bowl in Griffith Park. With just a couple of phone calls, Kiley and Lydia had arranged this impromptu picnic so that they could listen to Yellowcard without dealing with the crowds or the expense of buying scalped tickets.

Kiley heard the crowd roar as Yellowcard launched into

their hit "Ocean Avenue." She grinned, because it seemed almost as if they were cheering Lydia's love life. Lydia and Billy had finally done the deed. Successfully too, it seemed.

"Did you compare him to you-know-who?" Kiley asked.

"Luis? I told you, I'm not even counting Luis," Lydia insisted. "I will now and forever state that Billy Martin is the first boy I ever had sex with. And no one can prove otherwise." She opened the picnic basket and started extracting the plastic plates and wooden utensils that had been packed on the top. "Honestly, Kiley. When I was in Amazonia, I got the tribal shaman to blow some of that powder up my nose that they use for coming-of-age rituals. I used to consider my first time doing that the high point of my life. I thought I had turned into a crocodile. Not anymore."

Kiley laughed. "I'll take your word for it."

"Who's that psychologist guy, the one who said that sex was the root of all human behavior?" The plates and utensils out, Lydia went to work on the food.

"Freud, you mean?"

"Him. Yeah. You know, he was right. I don't know why the whole world isn't doing it all the time."

Lydia stretched languorously. In low-slung aqua short-shorts and a ribbed white tank top, she practically exuded sensuality in a way that made Kiley feel uncomfortable. She'd worn Target jeans and a faded brown T-shirt, and knew she exuded nothing. Maybe she should lose five pounds. Or ten.

God. How long had she been saying that?

"And then the third time—"

What? "You did it three times?" Kiley exclaimed.

"Nope. Four."

"Wow, I didn't even know that was possible."

Lydia leaned back on her tan, bare arms. "Of course it's possible. You just need to decide who you want to make it possible with. Tom or Jorge. Or both. At the same time, maybe."

Kiley blushed at the thought. "Don't you think it would help if I figured out who I wanted to be with before I have sex with either one of them?"

Lydia shrugged. "You could do a comparison test. Where is Tom, anyway? I thought he was back from Florida."

"We saw each other at the club, but we've been playing phone tag."

"You should be playing tag-team aerobics," Lydia opined. "He couldn't come tonight?"

"I called him. His older brother Tanner is stopping at LAX on the way home from Hawaii or something. He went to have a drink with him at Encounter."

"His loss." Lydia sniffed. "Anyway, Esme is coming with Tarshea and Jorge. So there'll be backup for you."

"Jorge isn't backup!"

"And Anya is straight."

Kiley was still chuckling when Billy, Esme, Tarshea, and Jorge—the other attendees at this impromptu picnic/rock concert—arrived at their picnic spot. They'd met down in the parking lot by Cahuenga and trudged up the steep hill together.

"This is fantastic!" Tarshea exclaimed, taking in the meadow. Dotted across the hillside were other picnickers on blankets. Some of them had come fully equipped with burning torches to provide illumination and lawn furniture for comfort.

"Nothing like it in Jamaica?" Jorge asked.

"No, mon!" Tarshea told him. "And no bosses to give me and Esme the night off, either."

"Well, welcome to America."

Lydia introduced Tarshea to Billy, and Kiley stood to offer him a hug. After hearing Lydia's description of the activities of the night before, it was kind of hard to make eye contact. She hugged Jorge, too, as a roar went up inside the Bowl. Yellowcard started "Inside Out."

"How often are there shows like this?" Tarshea asked Billy. She was wearing jeans and a gray blouse that Kiley recognized as belonging to Esme.

That was so thoughtful of her. Tarshea must have arrived without many clothes.

"About every other night," Billy told her. "Sting is playing next week. I think there's a reggae show toward the end of the month with Bunny Wailer."

"We must go," Tarshea declared. "That is the best music in the world."

Lydia was digging into the picnic basket and unpacking various containers. "Y'all have to taste the iced lobster thermidor. I asked Paisley to make it. She was so happy not to be cooking with Anya's tofu that she put together our whole meal basket. There's baby red potato salad, cold leek soup, noodles in stone-ground sesame paste, and a whole bunch of other stuff."

"I brought my mom's flan, but this kind of puts it to shame," Jorge said ruefully, nudging a Tupperware container with his forefinger.

"Don't go dissing your mama's cooking," Lydia chided as she passed around the covered dishes. "Hungry?" she asked Billy.

"Oh yeah." He kissed her.

The heat factor across the ground cover got a little intense, and Kiley looked away. She and Jorge locked eyes for a brief moment. His gaze was so warm, so welcoming. It would be so easy to be with a guy like him. When she allowed herself to think about it, she realized that the idea of sex with Jorge was not at all intimidating. She wouldn't worry about her thighs, or that her breasts were half the average Los Angeles cup size. He'd probably been with girls like her. Not like Tom, who probably only ever was with girls who were the physical equivalent of him. That is, drop-dead gorgeous. There'd been that statuesque Israeli model, with the black hair and violet eyes, Marym Marshall. They'd dated for a while. Kiley had even been to a party at her house. Kiley had felt like a troll in comparison.

Suddenly, she had to get out of there.

"Porta-Potties," she announced. Her eyes flashed Lydia the universal girl signal that meant: *Come with me.*

"That's code for girl talk," Lydia translated, scrambling up from the blanket. "We'll be right back."

Kiley winced. Did she have to be so obvious?

Esme raised her eyebrows as if to ask whether she should come along too. Kiley thought about it for a moment—Esme was so practical—but then decided it wouldn't be right to abandon Tarshea.

"We'll be right back," Kiley assured her.

They headed down the paved path to the Hollywood Bowl entrance four hundred yards away. As soon as they were out of earshot, Lydia bumped her hip into Kiley's. "So? Why the great escape?"

"I keep thinking about Tom."

"And I keep seeing how Jorge looks at you. Which makes him your official FBG," Lydia surmised.

"What's that?"

Lydia pushed some choppy blond hair off her cheek. "Fallback Guy—I read about them in *Jane*. When you have a guy who you're not sure is going to be your Main Guy, you need a Fallback Guy."

Kiley frowned. "I really like Jorge."

"That just makes you the kind of girl who can't admit that she'd use a boy," Lydia explained. "You've got morals or scruples or whatever."

Kiley almost laughed, and then took her friend's arm so that they could move out of the way of a small army of late-arriving picnickers heading up the hill to the meadow. "You say it like it's a bad thing."

"Until or unless you pledge your undying, monogamous love for either one of 'em, which is not something I recommend by the by, it is. Until the Main Guy pledges it back, I say have fun with both of 'em."

"Hold it. You didn't do that with Luis and Billy," Kiley pointed out.

"Actually I did."

"And you're sorry about it now."

"Hey. The Amas have a saying: If you see a wild boar in the jungle and you're hungry, don't be afraid to take a shot. The worst that can happen is you'll miss."

"I don't get it. You *are* sorry that you hooked up with Luis!" They reached the Porta-Potties. To her surprise, Kiley realized she really did have to go, and joined the short line.

"Don't confuse me with facts. Anyway, know who showed up at the restaurant where I ate with Billy last night?"

"Luis?"

"Yep. He claims it was a coincidence. I'm not so sure."

Kiley winced. "Was it horrible?"

"Nope. He was cool. He came in for a take-out order. No cut, no blood, no piranha attack."

The line edged forward. They stood behind a very pregnant girl baring her stomach happily in low jeans and a belly shirt. Sometimes it seemed to Kiley that everyone was more comfortable with their bodies than she was.

"So, what are you going to do about Tom and Jorge?" Lydia asked.

Kiley hesitated. "I'm not sure. I'm not even sure if Tom is that into me."

"You may be right," Lydia agreed, in her usual blunt fashion. "Which is why my advice is not to dump Jorge until you see if Tom is really interested. Because if Tom is out of the picture, Mr. Fallback could become Mr. Fall For."

14

"One love.
One heart.
Let's get together and feel all right!"

Esme stood in the doorway of the Goldhagens' family room in a state of stupefaction at the tableau before her. There were Easton and Weston, sitting on the carpet on either side of Tarshea as she played and sang the Bob Marley classic on a Martin acoustic guitar. Correction. The twins were singing, too. When the twins had learned "One Love" in English, Esme had no clue.

She'd awakened at her usual time, 7:30 a.m., so that she could get the twins up and feed them breakfast. Since Tarshea had arrived, she had accompanied Esme on her morning duties. It was fun to have her around. She was helpful, cheerful, energetic, and great with the kids. It also made a lot less work for Esme.

This morning, though, when she'd knocked on Tarshea's door, there'd been no answer. Esme figured that Tarshea was tired. But judging from this scene in front of her, Tarshea had gotten the twins up, dressed, and fed before Esme even turned off her alarm clock.

"Esme!"

Easton spotted her nanny, jumped to her feet, and ran across the room to give Esme a hug. She wore a pink T-shirt silk-screened with the faces of children of many races, under pink linen overalls. The outfit had been a recent gift from a young actress who'd met the twins aboard the *Queen Mary* for the final banquet of FAB.

"Did you hear sing?"

"I did," Esme said. Easton was making a real effort in English, even if the execution sometimes left something to be desired. "It was great."

"I sing, too!" Weston popped to her feet.

"I know, sweetie. You were both great." Esme swung her eyes to Tarshea, who was dressed simply in a pair of jeans and T-shirt. "Wow, you must have been up early. It's not even eight o'clock."

"Oh, it's nothing. I wasn't sleepy. I found this guitar in the home theater. I hope it's all right to play."

"It's Jonathan's," Esme explained. Jonathan had told her that when he was in ninth grade, he'd decided he was going to be the next Kurt Cobain. His dad had bought him this Martin beauty. The problem was, six months of daily lessons with the former lead guitarist for the Eagles left him no better than when he'd started. In the musical talent department, he'd been granted a zero. "He doesn't play anymore."

"We sing again! You too!" Easton dragged Esme toward the guitar, which Tarshea had propped against the couch.

Esme didn't resist. "Tarshea, tell me this: when did you have time to teach them?"

"Oh, just now. They are quick learners. Lovely voices, don't you think?"

"You fed them too?"

Easton answered for her. "Egg hats! We eated egg hats!"

"We ate egg hats," Esme corrected. Whatever the grammar, the meal sounded impossible, since the twins hated eggs in every possible way, shape, and form. Their breakfast was inevitably Honey Nut Cheerios.

"Oh, it's nothing. I toast a slice of bread and cut a circle out of the middle with the bottom of a glass," Tarshea explained. "Then I make a sunny-side-up egg and put it in the hole in the toast, and top it off with the toast circle. Egg hats. They are very big in St. Catherine parish in Jamaica, where I live."

"But—but the girls never eat eggs," Esme sputtered.

Tarshea shrugged. "I'm sure it's just that they like the cute little hats," she explained in her lilting accent. "It's how we got my little brothers to eat eggs, so I thought I'd give it a try."

"My beautiful babies!"

Diane Goldhagen appeared in the archway of the room and held her arms out wide to her two adopted daughters. Though the hour was early, she was already dressed and made up for the day in a white jacket adorned with a print of orange tree branches over a white cotton scoop-neck top and new skinny-legged jeans. All her old jeans—meaning, those purchased before the end of June—had just been donated to the Second Coming, a vintage store in the San Fernando Valley whose proceeds went to help HIV-positive women find gainful employment.

Neither daughter moved toward her. Instead, Easton stood by Esme, and Weston put her cheek against Tarshea's hand.

It was a sad moment. Esme could see in Diane's eyes how much her adopted daughters' reluctance hurt her. She was just about to tell them quietly to go and hug their mother, but Tarshea beat her to the punch.

"¡Si ustedes abrazan su mamá y la dicen que ustedes la aman, las daré un presente grande inesperado!"

Instantly, both girls bolted across the room and embraced their mother, babbling "I love you" in both English and Spanish.

Diane was overcome with joy. "What did you say to them, Tarshea?"

"Oh, just that they knew how happy they were to see their mama," Tarshea explained sweetly. "So there was no reason for them to hold back."

Esme was dumbstruck. That wasn't at all what Tarshea had said. Instead, she'd practically bribed them to hug Diane, promising them a big surprise present if they did. Diane couldn't understand a word of it, but Tarshea must have known that Esme would know. It was either an incredibly gutsy or incredibly foolish move. Esme wasn't sure.

"Mama, we sing with Miss Tee." Easton pointed to the guitar.

Tarshea grinned. "They made up a nickname for me. Miss Tee. I kind of like it."

"That's so darling!" Diane hugged the girls again. "Can you sing for me? I don't have much time, though. I have a meeting for a fund-raiser for the Spencer Jon Helfen Fine Arts gallery."

"Don't forget your spa appointment," Esme reminded her. "It's at noon."

Diane smiled. "Thanks for watching out for me, Esme."

"How about if we sing for your mother, girls?" Without waiting for a response, Tarshea got the guitar; counted off *uno, dos, tres, cuatro;* and then started to play. Instantly, the girls belted out the melody again.

> *"One love.*
> *One heart.*
> *Let's get together and feel all right!"*

Diane beamed and applauded. "That's so wonderful! I love Bob Marley."

"You sing too, Mama!" Easton instructed.

"All right." Diane walked over to her daughters, plopped onto the floor by them, and joined in. As she did, she helped the twins clap in time to the beat. All the while, Tarshea either sang along or grinned encouragingly.

Esme just stood there watching the warm family scene, feeling utterly and totally superfluous. Then, something else struck her: the shirt Tarshea was wearing, a red-and-white-striped V-neck. It was *hers*. By the designer Tocca, she'd bought it at Girl/Boy/Girl on an outing with Lydia.

Hoo boy. Tarshea had awakened the kids in Esme's charge, given them breakfast and gotten them to eat eggs, taught them a Jamaican song, and figured out a way to get them to tell their mother that they loved her. And she'd done it all while wearing Esme's shirt.

"Amazing," Tarshea murmured. "Simply amazing."

It was three hours later, and the four of them—the twins, Tarshea, and Esme—were spending the afternoon at the country club. Though they were stretched out on a couple of chaise lounges while the twins splashed in the shallow end of the pool, Tarshea's head swung around like a bobble-head toy on a bumpy road, taking in the rich, the famous, and the infamous.

Esme tried to see this environment through Tarshea's inexperienced eyes. When she did, the opulence became overwhelming. The men were all gym-buff and perfectly tan in surfer Jams; the women were all white and aggressively thin. They wore designer bikinis by Eres, Norma Kamali, or Armani Collezioni. No one appeared to have more on their mind than what they would order for lunch from the club's outstanding restaurant. Many were by their equally well-outfitted children, who themselves were almost always trailed by a nanny. Sometimes there were two nannies.

Although Jamaica was a resort island, Tarshea had confessed that she had forgotten to bring a swimsuit to America and couldn't afford a new one. Esme had been about to loan Tarshea her navy blue Nautica one-piece with white piping and crisscross white straps—she couldn't think about coming down on such a poor girl for borrowing a few items of her clothes without asking—but then just gave it to her outright. The gift had thrilled her.

"Dear Lord in heaven!" Tarshea grabbed Esme's arm. "*Coo yah!* Look there! Is that Tobey Maguire across the pool? My little sissy Margarita would die. They showed *Spider-Man* at our church."

Esme couldn't blame Tarshea for gawking. She'd wanted to gawk too, her first time at the club. But empathy could wait. In fifteen minutes, Weston and Easton had their swimming lesson. That was fine. That was better than fine. It would leave an hour for Esme and Tarshea to be alone, which meant that Esme could arrange for Tarshea to be alone, which meant that there would be time for Tarshea to be poached. As in, nanny-poached. As in, find the girl a job quickly. It was nice having Tarshea around, but sometimes she was too efficient.

"Miss Tee! Swim! Swim!" the twins called out as they splashed up and down in the shallow end of the pool.

Great. Esme couldn't help but notice that the girls were calling out for Tarshea and not for her. All the more reason to get Tarshea poached.

Fortunately, the twins' swimming instructor—a powerful young blond woman named Cally who spoke four languages—showed up early to spirit the girls away to the swim-instruction lane of the pool.

"We've got a half hour," Esme told Tarshea. "Let's get you poached."

"I still don't understand."

"Just follow my lead. We stand in the breezeway over there between the family pool and the adult pool, and wait for someone to approach. After you get hired, remember that."

"Remember what?"

"Remember that if your job isn't making you happy, you can always go to the breezeway," Esme explained.

Tarshea raised her eyebrows. "In Jamaica that kind of behavior means you are a drug dealer peddling ganja or you are a hooker peddling yourself. Dat is not me. I no smoke, I no drink, I no smoke ganja. I am a Christian girl."

"Not to worry, Tarshea." Esme was sympathetic. "It's just a job."

Tarshea hugged Esme. "You are a most wonderful friend."

Bullshit. She was not a most wonderful friend. She was a girl looking out for her own self-interest.

"Come on," Esme told her, and led Tarshea to the shady breezeway, where the club had recently ordered some redwood park benches. They sat together.

"Now what?" Tarshea asked.

"We wait."

They didn't have to wait long. Esme was looking down the breezeway toward the adults-only pool when she heard a familiar voice behind her. A nastily familiar voice. "Diane Goldhagen throw you out on your ass?"

Teetering toward her on five-inch mint green embellished satin wedges was Evelyn Bowers, the bony, high-strung publicist for the tobacco industry who was also known as the butcher of all nannies. She wore a yellow polka-dot bikini under a gossamer yellow tunic embroidered with beads. Her eyes were hidden behind sunglasses so large they made her head look pin-sized.

Kiley had actually worked for Evelyn briefly. Very briefly. Then, she'd come right back to this very breezeway to find another employer.

"Nope. I'm trying to help out my friend here."

"Really?" Evelyn moved closer and lifted her sunglasses above her eyes. "I happen to be looking."

Of course she was looking. She was always looking, because no one on planet Earth could stand working for her.

"I know you, and I know the nanny. I don't think it would be a very good match," Esme opined. Tarshea raised her eyes questioningly; Esme put a reassuring hand on her forearm.

"What, I'm not important enough? Is that it?"

"No, not at all—"

"And why can't your friend speak for herself?" Evelyn challenged.

"I can," Tarshea said simply. "If she assure me that it would be a bad romp for me to work wit' you, then it will not happen. I trust Esme."

Evelyn glared at Tarshea. "Well, when your next job turns out to be a disaster, don't come running to me, island girl. Remember that."

She wobbled off on her too-high heels back toward the family pool. As Esme watched her depart, she wondered if she'd just done the right thing and decided that she had. Much as she wanted Tarshea employed, she couldn't turn the poor girl over to Evelyn Bowers and look at herself in the mirror in the morning.

"Excuse me."

Someone sidled up to the bench. When Esme and Tarshea saw who it was, they could barely speak. It was Paula Abdul, her curvy body clad in a red raw-silk tank top and khaki shorts. Esme loved her on *American Idol*. She'd even thought about how much fun it would be to introduce the twins to it when the next season began.

Standing with Abdul was another tall and skinny Evelyn Bowers type, only with better hair and makeup. Her flowy white gauze dress fell from her bare shoulders and swooped gracefully toward the brick-inlaid path.

"I—I'm Esme. And I love your show," Esme said, feeling rather shy—which was a rare feeling for her. "I'm sure you hear that all the time."

"And I'm Tarshea. You're . . . the best!"

Paula smiled, and nodded to her friend to start talking.

"My name is Ann Marie Wolfenbarger, but I'm known as Ann Marie professionally," the woman said in a voice that was gentle and sonorous. "I design clothes. I'm not a member here, I belong to Riviera. Please just tell me to shut up if I'm being presumptuous. But Paula told me that if a nanny is looking for a new job, she comes right to where you two are sitting. Is that why you're here?"

Esme nodded. "That's true. But it's not for me. This is Tarshea. She's with me now at Diane Goldhagen's, watching Diane's children."

"The two girls from Colombia?" Ann Marie grinned. "I met them at FAB! Tarshea, do you think they would give you a good reference?"

"I think so, yes," Tarshea said softly.

"I know they will," Esme chimed in.

Ann Marie nodded. "Cool. Paula, do you have a pen?"

Paula extracted a yellow lollipop pen from her oversized cherry-print straw bag and gave it to Ann Marie. The designer scribbled down a phone number on the back of a business card and handed it to Tarshea. "Call me on my private cell this evening. Okay?"

Tarshea was so stunned and pleased that Esme had to answer for her. "Okay," Esme said, committing the number to memory.

The sooner, the better.

15

Anya and Kat stood by the kitchen counter and nodded with approval as they watched Martina hoist a heaping serving of broiled tofu and grilled vegetables onto her plate. Meanwhile, Jimmy stared aghast at his sister.

"Are you feeling okay?" He shook his head in disbelief.

Martina took a big bite, chewed thoroughly, and washed it all down with a large gulp of Rice Dream dairy-free milk. "Sure."

"But you hate tofu, you hate vegetables, and you're not big on Rice Dream, either," Jimmy reminded her. "What are you doing?"

"It's okay. I'm kind of hungry. You ought to eat more. It's really good."

Her eyes met Lydia's, who did her best to hide her grin lest the moms figure out that something was up. So far, Martina was living up to her side of the bargain. She was eating three meals a day of the allegedly good-for-you health crap that Paisley was preparing.

"This is last meal for Jimmy on low fat," Anya declared, with an authority that brooked no opposition. "Now that he is golfer he must create muscle mass. I will leave instructions for cook."

Lydia sensed a bonding opportunity. "You really should see Jimmy out there on the driving range. He has a lot of talent."

Anya nodded. "This is not surprise. His father was champion—"

"Anya, please."

Kat, who almost never interrupted her partner, cut off Anya's sentence. Lydia knew why. Though Jimmy and Martina had the same sperm donor, there was never discussion in the household of his identity. In an uncharacteristically sloppy move, Anya had been about to spill the beans.

"Our dad was a champion what?" Jimmy was on it immediately.

"Never mind," Anya replied. "I have not said anything."

"Was he a golfer?" Jimmy pressed. "Tiger Woods? Phil Mickelson? Sergio Garcia? Jack Nicklaus?"

"Jack Nicklaus is old man," Anya scoffed.

"They can freeze sperm. I read it on the Internet."

"Jimmy," Anya chided. "Enough. No sperm talk at dinner table."

Jimmy frowned, and then mashed a fork into a square of tofu on his plate. "I don't see why everyone else gets a mom and a dad and I can't even know who my dad is."

"It's not important. You have your mother and me."

Lydia felt for the kid. It wasn't exactly true that everyone he knew had both a mom and a dad. Many of the kids at the country club had single moms, since single momhood had become a very Hollywood thing. A few had single dads. More than a few had two moms or two dads. One kid lived in something called a polyamorous household—Lydia still couldn't figure out the mechanics of that arrangement. Still, she could understand how a boy in middle school would want to know about his father.

"Now we talk about training for Jimmy," Anya announced.

Training for Jimmy? He was a nonathletic kid who had finally found a sport he enjoyed. There was no need for him to treat golf like an Olympic event.

"Oh, I think the walking and swimming we do is probably enough," Lydia opined, then forked a mushroom slice into her mouth. Jimmy was right. This food made the roasted and salted earthworms of the Amazon seem tasty.

Anya gave Lydia the evil eye as only she could. "You are professional athlete now? You know correct training routine?"

"No," Lydia admitted.

"Anya is famous for her training regimens," Kat put in helpfully. "But . . . I think we can let Jimmy just enjoy golf, sweetie."

Anya sucked in her cheeks, clearly annoyed. "You are siding with nanny?"

"She's my niece," Kat said mildly. She stepped over toward the sink and took one of the glasses of iced green tea that Paisley had left out on a silver serving tray.

"Your niece lived in jungle. Here she is nanny. I am fitness expert," Anya insisted.

God, Anya was such a control freak. Back when she and Kat were rivals on the court, Anya had been famous for a training routine that put most male athletes to shame. She'd been interviewed on *60 Minutes* following her retirement, and had brought with her for show-and-tell a five-hundred-page loose-leaf binder. Each of her opponents since the age of fourteen was listed behind a separate tab, with entries consisting of her recollection of each match, the player's strengths and weaknesses, and a written game plan to insure her defeat. There was even one for Kat.

But she and Kat were no longer rivals; they were life partners. So the question was, Lydia mused, why did Kat put up with it? Maybe Anya ordered her around in bed and Kat liked it. Now that Lydia knew how much fun sex really was, she could understand how a girl might make a compromise or two while vertical to enjoy something truly excellent while horizontal.

Anya went into a monologue about the correct training regimen for a career in golf, which Lydia found beyond boring. Kat seemed to feel the same way, since she stared into her glass of iced tea as if it was some sort of oracle.

"Kat!" Anya boomed.

Lydia's aunt was so startled she almost dropped her tea. "What?"

"I am trying to teach children about excellence. Where is your mind?"

"Sorry," Kat murmured.

"Why must I be only parent who disciplines?"

"I discipline," Kat objected. "Maybe not the same way you do, but—"

"Is only one way," Anya insisted. "We are doubles team now, not hotshot singles."

Kat flushed. "Go on with what you were saying, Anya. I'm listening."

Lydia saw both kids slide down in their seats. They hated when the moms argued, and Anya was being particularly quarrelsome tonight. Then she remembered what Kat had said to her on the front porch: to please mention it to her if Anya did anything strange. Did this episode qualify? It didn't matter if it did, since it was happening not only in front of Kat but to Kat. Let her aunt deal with it.

She eyed the remains of her tasteless dinner. Enough with setting a good example. There was no way she was going to eat another bite of that mess.

"May I be excused?" she asked Anya. "There's an activity for Martina I need to prepare."

Anya tented her fingers. "What activity?"

"Some . . . hand-eye coordination exercises that I think will really help her with her tennis game," Lydia invented.

"You see, Kat. Even Lydia is on board." Anya nodded to Lydia. "Go ahead. I will send Martina out back when she has finished food on plate. Martina, sit up straight, no slouching!"

Lydia went into the bedroom of her guesthouse and lifted the Compton luxury mattress that had been installed the week before. Yep. The long flat cardboard box was just where she'd left it.

It hadn't been easy, organizing all the things she needed here in Beverly Hills. In the rain forest, you could find the stuff you needed just by scavenging in the jungle for a couple of hours. Anything else she could usually procure from the local shaman by trading him some of the precious cosmetics that she picked up in Manaus on her rare downriver trips to civilization. The shaman turned out to be a big fan of MAC lip gloss.

Nonetheless, she'd persevered—a branch of Home Depot had proved a gold mine. Not that the shaman would have approved of her improvisation, but sometimes a girl had to do what a girl had to do.

She carried the box into the living room just as she heard a knock on her front door.

"Martina?" she called.

"It's me!" the girl answered.

"You alone?"

"No!" Lydia recognized Jimmy's voice. "What are you doing?"

No way was Lydia involving Jimmy in this.

"It's a girl thing, Jimmy!"

"Aw, man," Jimmy moaned. "You and Martina are like this secret club. Why couldn't Momma Anya and Momma Kat have gotten me a guy nanny?"

"Because you have a girl cousin, not a guy cousin."

"It still isn't fair, Lydia. And you know it."

Jimmy was right. It wasn't fair. But Lydia didn't know what to do about it. Except, maybe . . .

"How about if I get one of my guy friends to hang out with you sometime, Jimmy? What would you think of that?"

Too late. Jimmy was gone. Martina reported through the door that he had gone up to the main house.

Lydia gathered the box up in her arms. Maybe she had lost her mind, agreeing to teach this to Martina. She was young, immature, insecure, and a whole list of other things that, from a logical point of view, made this venture less than wise. On the other hand, she was *her* cousin. There had to be some kick-ass genes in there somewhere.

She stepped outside and pointed to the hillside thicket of trees behind the moms' mansion. "Follow me."

For the next ten minutes, Lydia led Martina uphill into the woods.

"Where are we going?" Martina puffed. She stepped on a dead branch that lay across the narrow path; it snapped cleanly in two with a loud crack. Then she stepped on another. And another. The path was well littered with branches. Lydia had seen to that.

"You've never been up here?" Lydia looked over her shoulder at the struggling girl. Martina was in much better shape than she used to be, but she was still a big girl, clumsy with her size and shape, and she was still wearing one of her many oversized sweatshirts, which had to be hotter than hell. Lydia had on only cutoffs and a tank top as she scrambled up a path so narrow and twisting that a prize burro might have lost its footing.

"No."

"But it's right behind your house! You didn't go exploring when you were younger?"

Martina didn't respond this time, but just kept plodding along. "How much further?"

They stepped into a small clearing. Lydia put the long box down. "We're here."

"Thank God." Martina collapsed onto a bare log. "If you take me on this hike every day, I'll definitely lose more weight before school starts, even if I hate every minute of it."

"You can always come up here by yourself. Look around, sweet pea. What do you see?"

They were at the top of the wooded hill directly behind Kat and Anya's mansion, but the terrain was so steep that they'd had to walk nearly a mile to get there, with switchback after switchback. The secluded clearing itself wasn't more than twenty yards in diameter, and offered no view.

"Nothing," Martina reported.

Lydia nodded. She held her hair up and fanned the back of her neck. "Yep. Nothing. But if someone was coming up the path, you'd hear them long before they got here, because I put about a thousand branches down the last time I walked up here. Old Ama trick. Which makes this a perfect spot to explore the secrets of the rain forest. Open your box."

"Is it a blowgun?" Martina asked excitedly.

"Just open it."

She did, and the disappointment on her face was obvious. Instead of the long wooden tube that she must have expected, she found instead three pieces of white PVC piping of the type that a plumber might use to replace the leaking underside of a garbage disposal.

"That's not a blowgun."

Lydia had expected this reaction. "Wait and see," she counseled as she took the two-foot-long sections out of the box and started fitting them together into one long tube. At Home

139

Depot, they'd offered her piping that screwed together at the joints. This wasn't satisfactory for her purposes, so she'd special-ordered piping that fit together as seamlessly as a jigsaw puzzle.

"Is that what you used in the Amazon?" Martina asked doubtfully.

"Nope. We'd make ours out of this wood called *pucuna caspi*, which basically means good blowgun wood. It was a pain in the ass. You'd either have to hollow out a tube by burning it with a hot stake—that's a fun way to spend a week—or else go to the blowgun maker, who'd help you do it in sections and then glue and tie them together."

"Wow. You did that?" Martina's eyes were wide.

"More than once. But I think this PVC is better. Know what happens when a four-hundred-pound wild boar steps on something made of pucuna caspi?"

Martina moved her hands in a breaking motion.

"You got it. A week's work right down the old latrine, so to speak." Lydia held the PVC pipe up to her right eye and sighted straight down the line, imagining a fat squirrel monkey climbing one of the eucalyptus trees that circled the clearing. Yep. There were advantages to plastic, since it had none of the little imperfections, niches, and protrusions that almost always developed on a wooden blowgun no matter how meticulously it had been made. She tried to imagine what her Ama friends would think of a weapon made like this. Probably, they'd love it. Her shaman would probably embrace the thing and leave a MAC lip print on it.

"How does it work?" Martina asked impatiently.

"I'm getting to that." There was a second level to the box.

140

Lydia lifted out a sheet of cardboard. Underneath, nestled in bubble wrap so that they wouldn't bounce around, were about a dozen darts she'd made by hand. She'd actually started with top-quality dartboard darts from a game supply store, and then modified them.

The darts once had stabilizing fins, but Lydia had removed them, since her goal was to have no air pass around the outside when she fired the weapon. After the fins were gone, she glued the dart tip to a thin twenty-inch dowel, also courtesy of Home Depot. Then she fashioned a card-stock paper cone, shaped it so that it would fit perfectly inside the tube, and attached it to the dowel with superglue. The cone would catch the shooter's breath so that the dart could fly at maximum speed.

As Martina watched, fascinated, Lydia took one of the darts and inserted it into the blowgun, then tossed Martina an apple she'd stashed in the pocket of her cutoffs. "Put this on your head and go stand by that big tree."

Martina shook her head.

"You mean . . . you want to shoot it off my head?" she squeaked. "No way!"

"I'm just teasing you," Lydia admitted, laughing, although she knew she really could make the shot. "Put it on that gray rock."

She pointed to a boulder protruding from the dirt about fifteen yards distant. Martina complied, then quickly moved out of the way.

"When you aim, keep both your eyes open," Lydia instructed. "That's a big ol' beginner's goof. You can't hit anything sighting with just one eye."

Martina nodded solemnly. Lydia brought the blowgun to her lips and inhaled deeply. Then she blew out as fast and hard as she could. The dart whizzed out of the tub so fast it was nothing more than a blur.

"Wow!" Martina ran over to the apple and lifted it up. The dart tip had smashed right through its center. "That is so cool! Can I try it?"

Lydia felt a tingling of misgiving. "Only if you—"

"Only if I do it with you and keep it a secret—cross my heart and hope to die," Martina put in. "But can I please tell Kevin? Please, please, please?"

"Absolutely not."

Martina was crushed. "But that was the whole point."

"The point, sweetie, is for you to feel stronger and more powerful and more confident. If you aren't old enough to keep this secret then you aren't old enough to—"

"I know, I know. I promise."

Lydia handed Martina the blowgun. For the next half hour Lydia offered expert instruction, guiding Martina's hands, showing her where to look, how to focus and aim. Martina took a number of shots, and the last one came within a few feet of the apple, which was a big improvement from where she had begun.

"Okay. Gather your darts," Lydia instructed.

Martina scrambled around, looking for the darts. "But I want to practice more."

"Too dark. Time to go."

Her cousin protested, but when Lydia suggested how little fun it would be to negotiate the path down the hill in the dead of night, Martina moved swiftly. It didn't take long until they were back on home turf near the pool patio.

"If Momma Anya asks what hand-eye exercises we were doing, you're going to say we used magnetic darts and a dartboard," Lydia explained.

"Okay. This was the greatest, Lydia. I can't wait to go back and practice some more."

Lydia told Martina that it would be unfortunate if one of the maids was to uncover the weaponry in Martina's room during their daily cleaning. They wouldn't understand, and neither would Kat or Anya when the maid told them. Martina quickly saw the wisdom of what Lydia was saying, and was happy to relinquish custody of the box to her cousin. "But you'll let me take it out to practice?"

"If you follow my rules. Strictly."

"Thanks." Once again, Martina threw her arms around her cousin. "I love you, Lydia."

"Love you, too, sweet pea."

Lydia watched with a grin as Martina bounded off toward the main house, happier than she'd been all summer. Then she checked her watch: 9:15 p.m. Not too late. If Eduardo hadn't ruined Billy's evening by making him work late, there might still be time for him to pick her up for a hamburger and some extracurricular activities.

She went back to her guesthouse to call him, but found the doorstep blocked by an enormous envelope—five feet wide, four feet high, with her name scrawled in elegant calligraphy on the outside.

"Billy!" Lydia exclaimed.

Did the boy rock, or what? She had to turn the envelope on its side in order to open it; it held a card that was equally elegant and equally huge.

The presence of Miss Lydia Chandler
is requested this evening at Eleven pm
at the Buffalo Club
for late supper and cocktails

It was beautiful. It was romantic. It was thoughtful. Lydia would have been turning cartwheels of joy except for one thing.

It was from Luis.

16

"Hello. I'm Roger Goldman, and I'll be your scuba instructor here at the club for the next five days." Roger was cut from the cloth of Hollywood central casting: tall, buff, and blond. He even wore a red bandanna pirate-style on his head.

"Get ready for the time of your life," he continued, running a tan hand over his ripped six-pack, as if to make certain it hadn't disappeared in the last five minutes. " 'Cuz you're about to learn the greatest sport in the world that doesn't involve two people on a bed." He winked. "Scuba diving!"

Kiley figured Roger had done that intro-wink-thing a zillion times. Personally she found it beyond cheesy, but she noticed that Bruce had a huge grin on his face, as did the two friends he'd talked into joining him for scuba class. The guy was named Jerry—he proudly explained that he'd been named for the counterculture leader Jerry Rubin, whom his father idolized both in his hippie and capitalist periods. He had incredibly bushy hair and an enviable soul patch. The girl was named Sedah, and rolled her eyes when she explained that it was Hades spelled backward. Tall, model thin, and with skin the color of café crème, Sedah was the offspring of an aging British rock star who'd gone through more career transformations than Rod Stewart yet still managed to escape unscathed. He'd married a fashion model from Gabon, and Sedah was their only child. She looked great in a white bikini strewn liberally with real pearls.

"Okay," Roger went on, flipping through some permission slips on his clipboard. "Let me call roll, make sure no one's been eaten by the sharks in the pool."

Sedah laughed and batted her eyes at Roger. *Conquest number one,* Kiley thought as Roger called out the names on his list. His flirtations really didn't interest her, though learning scuba did. It was a crucial step toward her brilliant career as an oceanographer or marine biologist.

The night before, after the concert/picnic, she'd had the most vivid dream of her life. She was on a dive boat off some exotic island in the Seychelles. Tom was with her. They jumped off the dive boat hand in hand, and found themselves in an underwater wonderland. There was a sunken vessel on the ocean floor, but it wasn't a wreck—more like a life-sized version of the boats she used to float in her bathtub when she was a kid back in Wisconsin.

All around them, fish cavorted, and then two larger-than-life sea horses swam in their direction. Kiley knew what they had to do, which was to climb on the backs of these sea horses and go for an underwater pony express ride wherever the sea horses took them. That's exactly what they did, the fish following them in two long columns that finally merged into one.

The dream hadn't ended until Kiley's alarm clock sounded. Most of the time, Kiley staggered around the guesthouse like a zombie early in the morning because she'd never gotten used to the colonel's penchant for a pre-seven virtual reveille. Today, though, rising had been a pleasure. She'd been full of confidence. Maybe that dream had been her subconscious telling her that she and Tom were supposed to be together. Even before she'd had her first cup of coffee, she resolved to talk to Jorge very soon, to tell him they should stay friends, but no more. Anything else would be unfair. Thank God they'd parted last night with just a chaste kiss.

Once roll call had been completed, Roger asked all the students to get into the water and swim four laps in the Olympic-sized pool without touching the sides. Any stroke would be fine—he just wanted to check their endurance. Swimming was the only sport Kiley had ever really enjoyed. She passed this test easily. In fact, she was the first one done.

"You're a swimmer, I see," Roger commented as she climbed out of the pool and brushed water from her thighs and arms.

"A little."

Roger rubbed his abs again. "Then you'll love this."

Kiley wasn't sure if he meant his six-pack or scuba. Whatever. She had zero interest in him.

The other students all passed the swim test, too. When everyone had dried off, Roger showed an instructional video on a monitor that had been set up in a shady area just east of the pool. After the glitzy introductory beginning that Kiley thought looked quite a bit like some elements of her underwater dream, the class got a run-through of the equipment they'd be using. There were the oxygen tanks that would hold her air; the regulators that would deliver a specific amount of air with each breath she'd take; her mask; a snorkel so that she could breathe at the surface without lifting her head; plus weight belt, flippers, and more.

There was a lot to take in, but Kiley was tracking everything with a clarity of purpose she'd rarely felt before. From time to time Roger would stop the video, do some extra explaining, and then make eye contact to make sure that his students understood what they were watching.

Jerry's hand shot into the air.

"So yo, check it out," he began. "My mom is all freaked because she says this is like dangerous."

Roger brushed his own abs again. They were still there. "Actually it's an exceptionally safe sport. Way safer than, say, snowmobiling or skiing. Does your mom freak when you do those sports?"

"Oh yeah. But that's just how she is. She's already stressing about driver's ed."

"Well, tell your mom that the biggest issue with scuba diving is probably sunburn," Roger said.

"She slathers on the SPF five hundred," Jerry quipped.

The group chuckled, and Roger waited for the laughter to die down. "You're all going to be really well trained," he promised. "When you're forty feet down and you run into a problem, you need to keep your wits about you. Last time I checked, human lungs don't mix well with inhaled water."

Sedah laughed as if that was the funniest thing she ever heard, and swept her magnificent hair off her face in an obvious effort to get Roger's attention. It worked. He gave her a wink of her very own.

"Okay. Sedah and everyone else. You guys ready to get started?"

The class moved to the far end of the pool, where Roger had the equipment stashed in piles for each of his students. "First we're all going to suit up. Just like in the video. I'll come around and help everyone. Don't be shocked by how heavy your tank is. Once you're in the water, it'll feel weightless. When you're suited up, please sit on the edge of the pool."

Fifteen minutes later, the entire group had their gear on. Bruce and Jerry helped each other while Kiley and Sedah did the same. Meanwhile, Roger checked everyone's tank and equipment, spending a little extra time with Sedah. Then he slipped into the pool, wading into water up to his waist.

"This end of the pool ramps down toward deep water, obviously," he began. "One at a time, I want each of you to come in and walk toward the deep end. Put on your masks, but you don't need your flippers just yet. Put the regulator in your mouth, but don't turn it on. This is just for practice. Then, when I give you this signal, I want you to duck underwater like this." He made a downward motion with his palm, and then slipped underwater. A second or two later, he popped up again.

"Come on, man," Bruce exclaimed. "That's too easy. Let's get to the real stuff!"

"Tell you what, Bruce, when you want to be an instructor you can try to convince the certification board that you have a better way to teach," Roger suggested.

"Also known as: my way or the highway, Bruce baby," Jerry boomed, and everyone laughed again.

Bruce scowled. Roger pointed to him. "Okay, hotshot. You want to be first?"

"Definitely!" Bruce stood unsteadily under the heavy tank but made his way to the near end of the pool.

"Put the mouthpiece in," Roger counseled as Bruce stepped into the water. It reached his knees, his waist, and finally his chest. Roger motioned him down, and he slid underwater and popped up three seconds later.

He spit out his mouthpiece. "That's amazing. The tank doesn't weigh anything underwater."

Roger smiled. "Thanks for trusting me. Kiley, you and Sedah next. Side by side."

Kiley stood easily and then gave a hand to Bruce's friend to help her up.

"Mouthpieces in," she told the girl, feeling utterly confident. She couldn't wait until they got through this silly exercise and started to actually breathe air from the tank. She couldn't wait for her first real dive, outside the confines of this pool. There would be so much to see. Fish, porpoises, coral, lost wrecks from bygone eras—an entire universe. Her universe.

The water reached Kiley's knees, then her waist, and then the top of her tank suit. She saw Roger give her the okay sign. This was the moment Kiley had been waiting for her whole life. The beginning of something magic, something she had wished for and dreamed about. She had the hugest grin on her face when she ducked her head under the surface water.

The feeling came over her in waves: dizzy and woozy, then nauseated. The pool was whirling, her head buzzed, her heart pounded. She couldn't—couldn't breathe. She felt her knees buckle. . . .

"Kiley! Kiley!"

Her name was being called from far away. She opened her eyes. She was prone on the concrete next to the pool. Roger was looking down at her with concern in his eyes; the rest of the class formed a ring around them.

"Wha-what happened?"

"You blacked out," Roger told her, checking her pulse. "You feeling okay?"

Blacked out? How was that possible?

"I'm okay . . . I think." She saw Bruce and his friends just behind Roger and managed to wave at him in what she hoped was a reassuring gesture.

"You taking any medicine? Under a doctor's care? Eat anything strange?"

Kiley shook her head. "No, nothing. Bruce had the same thing I did for breakfast. Juice, cereal . . ."

"Man, if you tell my mom about this my ass is grass," Jerry quipped. Kiley laughed weakly, which helped to break the tension.

"Well, your pulse is okay, Kiley," Roger announced, "that's good news." He turned to the other students. "Let's take fifteen, you guys. Out of the tanks, go get some water." He checked his Casio dive watch. "Back here at twelve-forty-five. Kiley, you rest right there."

The instructor waited for the class to scatter before he spoke to her again. "How are you feeling now?"

"Fine." Kiley sat up.

"Ever fainted before?"

Kiley shook her head. "Nope. I have no idea . . . I feel great. Normal."

"Good. Because I'm going to walk you back into the water, and we're going to do it again. Just you and me. Forget about what happened before. Could be as simple as the temperature difference on your skin between the cold water and the sun shocking your system. So, you ready?"

Kiley nodded and stood. She was utterly baffled about what had just happened to her and was utterly determined to do it right this time.

She and Roger walked to the near end of the pool, and started down its gentle slope toward the deep water. The cool water reached her knees, her waist, and again the top of her swimsuit.

"You good?" Roger asked.

"I'm fine."

"Okay then, mask on."

Kiley put her mask on. So did Roger.

"Regulators in."

They put in their mouthpieces. Once Roger saw that Kiley's was securely in her mouth, he made the same downward motion with his arm. Kiley sank beneath the water.

Oh God.

It happened again. She was dizzy and nauseated. She couldn't breathe. She felt as if she was going crazy, or dying. Her heart pounded. It was horrible, the worst thing she had ever experienced in her life. It took all her will to push up so that her head was out of the water before she passed out again.

She ripped off her face mask, panting, gulping for air, trying hard not to cry. "I—I don't—"

Roger put a comforting hand on her shoulder. "Kiley, have you ever heard of panic disorder?"

No, it couldn't be. *Please God, don't let me have it.*

"Kiley?" Roger prompted.

"My mother." Kiley's voice was flat. "She gets panic attacks."

Roger nodded. "Maybe there's some genetic basis for it. Something in your family."

"I can't have it. My mother is . . . she's afraid of everything and I'm . . . I swim all the time. I swim underwater. Why should I get an attack when I've got the gear on, and not when I don't have it on?"

"When you're swimming underwater you know you can surface at any time. In your gear, you might be fifty feet down. Or sixty. Or deeper. So even though you weren't deep now, psychologically . . . maybe you were."

Kiley realized she was crying, salty tears mixing with the chlorinated water on her face. She fisted them away. How could she hope to study the ocean if she couldn't submerge in scuba gear? What a joke. She looked up. Bruce and his friends had gathered at the edge of the pool and were staring at her with concern. Or maybe it was pity—the same pity that she had felt for her own mother so many times.

"Talk to your doctor," Roger recommended. "You're not the first person to discover it the hard way. And better here in the pool than out on the ocean."

"Thanks. I guess I'm done for the day, huh?"

"Yeah."

She trudged out of the pool with the gear she feared she might never wear again, wondering whether she was not just done for the day, but done for life.

17

"Good evening, and welcome to my humble abode."

Beverly Baylor bowed low with a theatrical flourish, and then enveloped Esme in a bear hug as if they were long-lost friends, instead of two people who'd crossed paths at the Craft Services tent on a movie set a few days before. Esme suffered through the embrace. Where she had grown up, there were friends and there were strangers. Beverly was definitely a stranger.

The soap opera business had been good to the movie star. She lived in a white, ultramodern house on Tenth Street in Santa Monica that she currently had up for sale. Esme had tarried at the For Sale sign on her way to the front door, and extracted a one-page dossier about the house. It was a knock-down property built in the mid-1990s, which meant that Beverly had purchased a previous house on this same plot of land and knocked it down to build this one. With five bedrooms, high ceilings, windows that soared toward the roof, and a backyard spa and patio, Beverly was asking a cool 3.4 million dollars. Beverly herself was bathed in the soft yellow light of her entryway. She wore a lavender silk peasant shirt, tiny purple shorts, and leather lavender-beaded sandals. It was an outfit that would have been appropriate on a woman half Beverly's age, even if the star did have the surgically adjusted body to make it work.

Esme had been surprised when Beverly had called her the morning after her visit to the movie set and begged for a tattoo appointment even before the Chinese one was lasered into oblivion. The actress explained that she wanted cowboy-style body art on her inner thigh, since the current love of her life was rodeo champ Maverick Saturn. They had been dating for three months. Beverly had confided details of startling intimacy, such as when and where they had first had sex (third date, in the stables at Will Rogers State Park). Why the inner thigh? Beverly wanted to mark the spot that her cowboy loved to kiss the most. When Esme pointed out that Maverick might not be thrilled by the idea of smooching his own image, Beverly giggled and suggested that would not be a problem for this particular Wyoming cowboy.

Way too much information.

Esme had invited Jonathan to join her, but just as he had been all week, he was shooting back in Topanga Canyon. She'd left the twins with Tarshea; they were screening *Bruce Almighty* for the zillionth time in Steven and Diane's home theater. At least she could breathe easy now that Ann Marie and Tarshea had hit it off nicely at the club. Tarshea had called to set up the interview, in fact. Surely she'd get the job. She was a great girl, and was going to make Ann Marie a fabulous nanny.

Beverly ushered Esme inside. The front entryway opened to an enormous family room that Beverly bragged had just been redone in a southwestern motif. A brown leather sofa with an elk skin thrown over the back dominated the room, along with camel chairs in the shape of riding saddles. There was a free-standing twenty-foot stone fireplace. Above it was a rack of antique firearms and a mounted elk's head that presumably once belonged to the creature whose skin was currently adorning the sofa. Cowboy art and photographs from the Old West covered the walls, including an enormous depiction of the Boot Hill cemetery in Tombstone, Arizona. Esme got close enough to read one of the epitaphs on a headstone. "Here lies Lester Moore. Four slugs from a .44—no Les, no more."

"I redecorated for Maverick," Beverly gushed, "and I just adore, adore, adore it. It's so earthy. He shot the elk. Look at this picture."

She pointed to the far wall, where there was yet another oversized framed photograph. This one was of a rangy blond guy in a cowboy hat, chaps, and vest, along with the actress herself. Beverly was entwined around him, as naked as Maverick was clothed. He looked to be about twenty-five.

"Isn't he delicious? He's going to do a guest run on my soap in the fall, as a mysterious cowboy who comes to town and steals my heart because I have amnesia and don't remember my husband and three children. So, come meet the girls. Girls!"

The actress called toward the kitchen, and two women approximately her age marched out into the family room.

"The artist!" a very blond woman cried, clapping her

hands. She was even skinnier than Beverly, and wore a tight black miniskirt, white tank top, and thigh-high boots with Lucite stiletto heels.

Beverly did a quick introduction. The blond was Kirsti and proudly announced that her husband was a full partner at Endeavor. The redhead was Elena, a regular on another ABC soap. She was another size nothing, with wavy, glossy hair and cheekbones that could cut glass. On her left ring finger was a diamond the size of a golf ball. She waved it in Esme's direction. "We've heard so much about you."

Beverly motioned toward her two friends. "Oh darling, you're going to do everybody. That's what makes it so fun."

"Botox parties are so last year!" Kirsti laughed.

Now Esme understood. This was to be a tattoo party, though no one had bothered to inform her. She did some quick arithmetic. If she did all three women, it could take four or five hours. Maybe longer. At the rates that Jonathan had quoted, she could leave with . . . well, a shitload of money.

Still, she felt a professional obligation to set them straight before she got down to work. "It takes at least a couple of hours to do a really good tattoo. Longer, if you want me to do it freehand."

"Oh poo, that doesn't matter. We've got all night." Kirsti grinned and then reached for a bowl of shelled macadamia nuts on Beverly's coffee table. She brought a fistful of nuts nearly to her mouth, and then smacked her right hand with her left hand. "Bad hand. Very bad. No nuts for you!"

"Don't be so obsessive, Kirsti," Elena advised. "You probably haven't eaten all day."

"Not true. I had a granola bar for breakfast," Kirsti defended herself.

Beverly plopped herself down next to Esme. "I'm first, since it's my house. But I'm assuming you're not in a rush. We brought our checkbooks."

"I actually have cash," Elena put in.

Well then. Cash and checks. Time to get to work.

Esme opened her box and set out her tools. As she got everything ready, Beverly's elderly Latina maid came in with a tray of beverages ranging from iced tea to Campari to a pitcher of cranberry martinis. She caught Esme's eye and flashed a barely discernable wink of solidarity.

Esme smiled back. "Could you please put some water on to boil?"

"I have it already," the maid replied. "From the tea. I'll get it for you."

"In a bowl, thanks. Boiling. I need it for sterilization."

"And the appetizers, please, Anna," Beverly instructed. "Thank you! Esme, dear, where do you want me? I've set up lights in the conversation pit, if that would help."

"That would be fine."

There was a conversation pit at the far end of the living room. Beverly deposited herself on the second step, lifted the bottoms of her short-shorts, and pointed one bubble gum–pink finger at the very top of her right thigh. "That's where I want it."

"You're really sure you want your boyfriend to be looking at himself when he kisses you there?" Esme couldn't help herself. It was so much tougher to undo a tattoo than to apply one.

Her friends roared with laughter at some inside joke as Esme went through her pre-tattoo sterilization routine. Fortunately, the star was a fan of bikini wax, so there were few stray hairs on her upper right thigh.

"You make my work easier," Esme told her.

"Oh honey, we all get the Brazilian wax at Pink Cheeks in Sherman Oaks," Beverly said.

"Well, I have to shave you anyway." Esme had no desire at all to shave Beverly Baylor's anything, but wasn't about to skip any of the hygiene steps. People treated the acquisition of a tattoo like a visit to the makeup department at Fred Segal— something to do for kicks. But Esme knew tattoos were equally art and serious business. An infection could ruin your whole year.

Beverly leaned back to give Esme better access to her skin. "Shave away. But I'm warning you. Paparazzi have been known to pay my neighbors to climb in their trees and shoot with a telephoto lens. They'll say we're having a mad affair, Esme. Think about how high you want to go."

Ten minutes later, Beverly's friends had put a U2 CD on her sound system, Anna had brought in a plate of vegetarian appetizers with little caloric content, and Esme had finished her preliminaries. "So, what do you want, Beverly? A cowboy? A cowboy on a horse? Neck and shoulders? Full-length?"

"Definitely full-length, from what I've heard," Kirsti snickered.

"Absolutely," Beverly agreed.

"How big?" Esme asked.

"Very!" Elena cried, a comment that elicited more peals of

laughter from a group that Esme was liking less and less by the minute.

"I meant the tattoo."

"Oh . . . this." Beverly held her hands about five inches apart.

"Someone, bring me some paper and a pencil," Esme ordered. "I want to get this right. A cowboy on a horse, right?"

"Right. Anna! Bring paper and pencil to Esme, please! From my art room!"

A moment later, the maid appeared with a full-fledged sketch pad and charcoal art pencil and handed them to Esme, who had gone to the photograph of Maverick in order to get a good look at the structure of his face. Only then did she sketch.

Magically, a profile view of Maverick appeared. He was on a gray horse, flinging a lasso toward an unseen target.

"How'll that be?" She showed the sketch to her client as the music shifted to a techno band that Esme didn't recognize.

The soap star gazed at the sketch. "It's . . . perfect. I love it. Don't you love it, girls?"

Kirsti and Elena gathered around their friend, nodding approvingly. "You're a very talented girl," Elena declared. "I'll wait all night for you to do me."

Once again, the three women exploded in laughter. Esme just gritted her teeth.

It's a job, she reminded herself. *Remember how much they're paying you. You don't have to like them to do it well.*

"Okay, let's get started. This is going to hurt somewhat," Esme warned. She turned on her needle, and got her containers of ink in easy range.

"Oh honey, I had three glasses of wine before you got here so I won't feel a thing," Beverly insisted.

Esme took a deep breath. Then she cut into the flesh of Beverly's thigh.

"Fuck!" Beverly shrieked.

"The needle doesn't penetrate very far. But there are a lot of nerves close to the surface," Esme explained.

"I'm not a rookie," Beverly fumed. "My back didn't hurt half this much."

"Remember the vino," Kirsti coached.

The actress gritted her teeth. "Okay, bring it on, Esme. I've had worse. Kirsti, no vino. Martinis."

Esme applied the needle again, methodically creating the cowboy's silhouette sitting astride a horse, and then the ring of the lasso.

"I know this isn't your fault, Esme. But could you please hurry up?"

"No. But I could stop and finish another time," Esme offered. The outline was complete, but it would take at least another hour of concentrated work to fill in the details and add all the colors.

"No, no, no." Beverly drained another martini and called for more. "You and Jonathan must be into pain."

Esme ignored the jibe. "Red shirt okay for the cowboy?"

Beverly nodded. Fortunately the alcohol was having a cumulative effect on the actress, who was no longer bellowing every two minutes.

"Yeah. We hear you hooked Jonathan Goldhagen," Elena noted as Esme continued to work. "Lucky you."

"Maybe lucky him," Esme said lightly. She was sick of

people telling her how fortunate she was, as if she was some-how not worthy of Jonathan.

"How did you meet him?" Elena asked. She speared a freshly broiled shrimp from the ceramic platter on the coffee table.

"Oh, you know," Esme said vaguely, blotting another drop of blood from Beverly's thigh. She wasn't about to tell these women that she was the Goldhagens' nanny. She owed them nothing more than excellent work.

Finally, the cowboy's shirt was done. She switched to brown ink for his chaps.

"Word to the wise," Beverly advised as Elena poured her yet another drink. "Watch out for Mackenzie. The girl can be vi-cious. I was in wardrobe yesterday and she gives me these jeans that a two-year-old couldn't fit into. When I complained, she said I must have put on weight because according to the measurements she did before we started shooting, the jeans should fit. Bitch."

Esme kept her face impassive and the needle steady in her hand. Inside, though, she fumed. Jonathan's ex-girlfriend was working on his movie and he'd neglected to mention it to her?

"Who's Mackenzie?" Elena asked.

"Jonathan's ex," Esme filled in, before Beverly could reply, then gave her subject a cocky look. "I'm not worried."

That was a lie, of course. Why hadn't Jonathan told her? Did he have anything to do with her getting the job? Probably not, but what if? Esme forced herself to concentrate on finish-ing the chaps, and then the gray steed. She'd had him rear up on his hind legs. She was careful to show his musculature—the flanks, the taut body.

"Amazing." Elena peered closely at Beverly's thigh. "This girl is a genius."

"I want to see!" Beverly started to hunch over as if she was in a yoga class, but Esme stopped her with one hand. She'd been at it for close to three hours. That was six hundred bucks right there, and there was still more to do.

"When I'm done. Stay still." She went back to the cowboy's face to add some detail. "How did you know Jonathan and Mackenzie used to be a couple?"

"Oh, honey, Mackenzie tells everyone they're still a couple. That's why I was so surprised when I met you on the set."

"I got it covered," Esme insisted, her voice terse. She worked in silence for the next fifteen minutes, letting banal conversation swirl around her. She really didn't care who did the best foil weaves or the best caviar facials or whatever other stupid thing was on the minds of these women. She had a job to do.

"Okay," she told Beverly, when she'd inked a bit more on the lariat to correct the color. "Look."

Esme held out her mirror. The actress peered at her thigh's reflection.

"Oh my God, I adore it!" she shrieked.

All the women agreed—Esme was spectacular, brilliant, fantastic. The praise went on and on as she carefully blotted the last of the blood and wrapped the tattoo in fresh gauze.

"So who's next? Me?" Elena asked as Beverly wrote a check and handed it to Esme. It was for eight hundred dollars. Seven hundred for three and a half hours' work, plus a hundred as a tip.

"Fill in your own last name, I can never remember it," the soap actress instructed.

Esme had been planning to do all three tattoos this evening, even if it meant she wouldn't get to sleep until well after midnight. Now, though, she realized how tired she was. "I've got to go," she told Kirsti and Elena.

Kirsti whipped out her Treo 700W, and Elena did the same with a Palm Pilot. "What's your first free date?"

"For both of us," Elena chimed in.

"I—I don't know," Esme stammered, marveling that she'd just made eight hundred dollars for three and a half hours' work. It was more than what the Goldhagens paid her for a full week.

"Tell you what. I'll give you a deposit now," Kirsti declared. "All I ask is that you fit me in as soon as possible. First available."

Elena thought that was a wonderful plan as well. Moments later, Esme was holding their checks for three hundred and fifty dollars each. That made fifteen hundred dollars. She got all their numbers, gave Beverly instructions on the care of her new tattoo, and then was escorted by all three women to her Audi. With profuse and somewhat drunken thanks, they bid her farewell.

Esme climbed into the Audi and headed for the Goldhagens'. She couldn't figure out which was the stronger emotion: the giddy feeling of knowing that she had just become an overpaid tattoo artist to the stars, or the discomfort at what Jonathan wasn't telling her about Mackenzie. On a whim, she turned right at the corner of Twenty-sixth and San

Vicente instead of continuing east toward Bel Air. Jonathan's apartment wasn't far from there—maybe ten minutes' drive in the opposite direction. That was worth the investment of time and energy. She was going to get to the bottom of this. Right now.

18

"I want you, too. So much."

Lydia, who was stepping past the moms' half-open doorway on her way to Martina's room, stopped dead in her tracks.

"Taste my lips." Anya's voice was unmistakable.

Taste my lips?

"Take off shirt."

Take off shirt? Who was she talking to? It couldn't be Kat, since her aunt was swimming outside in one of the two new continuous wave tanks that had been installed out by the pool.

"I want to lick nipples. This is favorite spot for me."

There was very little of a sexual nature that could gross Lydia out. However, hearing Anya discuss nipple licking—she pronounced it "leeking"—was right up there. She snuck a quick glance through the barely open door. It was a risky move, she knew. What if Anya saw her? What if there was someone else in the room with her? Unlikely, since she'd heard neither a response nor the sounds of shared ardor. Probably Anya was on the phone.

"Now you take off everything."

Lydia peered in, but couldn't see a thing besides Anya's splayed legs on the bed. Meanwhile, Anya's side of the conversation got hotter and hotter. Who knew that a woman this rigid and overbearing could come up with some of the stuff she was saying?

"Now I do this." Anya sighed with pleasure.

Dang. Just to be absolutely positive that the moms weren't spicing up their marriage with dirty talk, Lydia ran downstairs and out the back entrance toward the pool deck. Yes. Just as she'd thought, Kat was doing an aggressive crawl in the larger wave tank. Her rhythm was strong, as if she'd been in there for a while.

Lydia hustled back upstairs.

"Oh yes. It is hot on phone with you. Yes. Do more, do more."

This was not good. There was no accounting for taste, but her aunt loved this stone-hearted bitch. Was Anya cheating with Oksana, the gorgeous young Russian professional tennis player whom she coached? That was possible. Oksana had even hit on Lydia when she'd first arrived in America. Yep. Oksana could definitely be the one. Then Lydia realized she couldn't be the one. If Oksana had been the one on the other end of the phone, Anya would most likely be speaking in Russian.

Kat had asked her point-blank to let her know if Anya was

doing anything out of the ordinary. This qualified, yes. But just because Kat asked didn't mean that Lydia had to parachute into the middle of what could be a big ol' dung heap.

Kiley lay on her back and stared at the ceiling of her guest-house bedroom.

It had been a brutal afternoon. She could only sit poolside and observe as Roger led the scuba class through its first in-the-water exercises. Her classmates had drifted by to offer their support, but Kiley felt sure that what they were feeling was not compassion, but pity. She knew this because of how many times she'd pretended to feel compassion but actually felt pity during her mother's panic attacks. The knowledge of how she'd acted then made her feel even worse now.

At least Bruce hadn't even bothered to fake his kindness. All he said was, "Tough break, but I'm staying in the class. I've waited a long time to try to get something going with Sedah." He also added, regarding Kiley's inability to complete even one underwater dunk: "Damn, the colonel's gonna be pissed. Better you than me."

Maybe she shouldn't have expected more from a kid who'd been raised by an insane alcoholic rock star. All Kiley had asked was that Bruce let her be the one to tell the colonel. Bruce was fine with that. If he didn't say anything, he couldn't get blamed.

Kiley had endured the day at the club, dinner with the colonel and the rest of the family, and even an hour of the Los Angeles version of Monopoly (Rodeo Drive taking the place of Boardwalk) with Serenity, Sid, and Susan. Susan cornered the market on the most expensive properties, but let Serenity win anyway. Fortunately, the colonel opted not to play. He wouldn't have given an inch to his sister-in-law's kids, and would have made Kiley a nervous wreck to boot.

After the game, the kids went to bed and Kiley hurried back to her guesthouse. There was only one thing on her mind: to call her mother. She hadn't talked to her since the escaped prisoner episode, which was a good sign. As she pressed speed dial, Kiley could picture the scene in the McCann living room. Her mom in the brown faux-leather easy chair watching sitcom after sitcom; her dad already passed out on the couch with the fallout of a six-pack littering the floor in front of him.

Scripps was supposed to take her away from that life, Kiley thought. That the thing she loved most, the ocean, incited panic attacks made her want to cry. How could her dream die just when it was beginning?

She went over and over everything that had happened at scuba class that morning, and kept coming to the same sickening, heartbreaking conclusion: Somehow she had inherited her mother's anxiety attacks. Could it possibly be genetic, like a tendency toward diabetes or breast cancer?

"Hello?" Maybe it was a result of having been in Los Angeles, but her mom's Wisconsin accent sounded even flatter than usual.

"Hi Mom. It's me. Don't worry, I'm fine," Kiley added automatically, as she had been doing since she was a kid. Any little thing could launch her mother into panic mode.

"Oh good, sweetie. It's so good to hear from you. They caught those crazy criminals an hour after we talked. I'm back to work. How are things out there in crazy California?"

Kiley was careful to keep her voice upbeat and perky. "Good, Mom. Really good."

"I've been wanting to ask you. What about school in the fall? I can't believe my baby is going to be a senior in high school. Are you registered?"

"Yep."

This was true. The week before, the colonel himself had accompanied her to Bel Air High School to vouch for her eligibility to attend the school. As it turned out, no vouching was necessary. The entire administrative office at BAHS had been following the saga of Platinum and her children, and knew who Kiley was. They'd registered her in short order.

"That's great, Kiley." Her mother's voice was quiet and sincere. "I'm so glad you're following your dream, honey. That's what I want for you."

Kiley gulped hard. "I know, Mom."

"What else is new? I was a mess last time we talked, I know."

No kidding.

Quickly, Kiley told a couple of funny stories about the colonel and the children that made her mother laugh. Then, she shifted into the real reason for her call. "Mom, can I ask you something?"

"Sure, sweetie."

She realized that her hands were sweating profusely. "I was just wondering . . . could you tell me when you first had one of your attacks?"

Silence.

"Panic attacks, you mean?"

"Yeah."

"Oh, Kiley." Her mother sighed. "Did you—"

"No, no, Mom. Not me," Kiley said hastily. "A friend."

She squeezed her eyes shut and felt tears leak out anyway. How could she possibly tell her mother the truth? Her mom, who had given up on her own dreams. Her mom, who had allowed Kiley to stay in California alone, so that Kiley could follow her dream. For both of them, she had told her daughter.

"Kiley McCann." Her mother's voice was low and intense. "I did not raise my daughter to be a liar and we have been down this road before. I warn you, do not lie to me. It's you, isn't it?"

She nodded glumly, and then realized that of course her mother couldn't see that. "Yeah," she whispered. "It's me."

"Tell me what happened, Kiley. I have a lot of experience with this."

Kiley got off her bed and paced. "It happened today. In the pool. When I first went underwater in a scuba diving class. It was horrible. I felt like I was dying."

Just those five sentences made Kiley's stomach roll over.

"Oh, honey . . . I feel so bad for you. First your grandmother, then—"

"What?" Kiley had never even met her maternal grandmother, who'd died before she was born. "You never told me that!"

"Why put it in your head? Besides, you've always been so fearless, Kiley. You were such an independent little girl. I thought you were immune."

"When did hers start, do you know?"

"When she was a teenager. That's what she told me."

Kiley felt like barfing. She already knew that was when her mother's problems had started, too. She sagged back onto her bed. First her grandmother, then her mother, then her. If she had a kid, she'd probably pass it down too. What a gift of the generations.

"I feel terrible for you, Kiley. It's my fault—"

"Of course it's not your fault," Kiley insisted wearily.

As her mother went on, sharing a detailed history of her teen experiences with panic disorder, somehow Kiley felt the stirrings of a new resolve. There had to be some way to beat this. Her mother had never taken anything but ineffective herbal remedies because she had been raised a Christian Scientist.

"There are doctors who specialize in this, you know," her mother was saying. "And medications."

Medications? Had her mother, who didn't even take aspirin, just said *medications*?

"But Mom, you—"

"Kiley, you are not me. I don't want you saddled with this." Her mother's voice was firm and loud in her ear. "You go to that good university and find a doctor who specializes in this. Do you hear me?"

"UCLA, you mean."

"Yes. Make an appointment with the best doctor you can find. Do whatever you have to do, Kiley."

Kiley was taken aback. She'd never, ever heard that kind of steel in her mother's voice.

"I will," she promised.

"And try not to worry. Worrying makes it worse. Besides,

maybe it won't be as bad for you as it was for my mother and me."

After sharing "I love yous," they hung up. Kiley lay back on her bed again, contemplating the same spot on the ceiling as before she'd phoned home.

Maybe it won't be as bad for you as it was for my mother and me.

That could be true. Maybe it wouldn't get as bad as with her mom, for whom every little thing outside her comfort zone—from a late taxicab to a room key that didn't work to escaped convicts in Chippewa Falls—could set off a full-bore anxiety attack.

There was, of course, another possibility. Maybe it would get worse.

"Aunt Kat?"

Kat looked up from the kitchen table, where she was doing prep work for her upcoming broadcast of the U.S. Open for ESPN. All across the table, she'd set out small cutouts of tennis courts, along with file cards listing the matches that would take place on those courts, and at what time. As Lydia looked in, she realized how much effort Kat put into her career. It broke Lydia's heart to have to say to her aunt what she was about to say.

"Yes, Lydia? I hope this is important. I'm trying to keep fifty-six matches straight here."

"It is." Lydia stepped into the kitchen and leaned against the marble counter. She already knew this conversation was going to suck. But after thinking about it long and hard, she'd decided that her loyalty was to her aunt, who deserved to know the truth about the cheating bitch she'd married.

Unless, of course, she already knew, which would make this conversation a mega-embarrassment to all involved. Shit. There was no way out.

Kat smiled thinly. "You look as if someone died. Hopefully it's not that bad."

"No one died," Lydia assured her. "But . . . it's bad."

"You're pregnant," Kat guessed.

"Lord no!"

"Okay. You've got my full attention anyway. Go." Kat closed the black loose-leaf binder that was directly in front of her.

"Remember what you told me a few nights ago—I mean, remember what you asked?" She could barely get the words out. "About . . . Anya?"

Kat nodded.

Suddenly, Lydia realized that one of the children, or even Anya, could come waltzing into the kitchen in the middle of this conversation. She slid into the chair closest to her aunt.

"Something happened. Something weird."

Kat turned her palms up. "Enough with the melodrama, Lydia. Just say it."

Lydia did, in one long monologue that began with her walking past the open doorway of the moms' bedroom and ended with her verifying that Kat hadn't been at the other end of the call. She tried to avoid giving a sentence-by-sentence repetition of what she'd overheard, but Kat wanted details. So Lydia ended up recounting the one-sided conversation as best she could.

Kat paled, which meant that Anya's phone sex wasn't anything that she knew about. Lydia felt horrible that she'd been the bearer of such shitty news. Here was a perfect example of

175

why people shouldn't get all bent out of shape about sex. If you just thought of it as a recreational sport, you couldn't get your heart broken. Of course, if Billy had sex with someone else, she might have to do the girl serious bodily harm. Lydia knew this was illogical, but she didn't care.

"Do you have any idea who was on the other end of that conversation, Lydia?"

"No. I thought maybe Oksana?" Lydia guessed. "That's not based on anything except that she hit on me right after I arrived. Of course, if it had been Oksana, wouldn't they have been speaking Russian?"

"Oksana hit on my straight-out-of-the-jungle-teen niece?"

"Oh, it makes no nevermind. I'm the adventurous type. But you—"

"I'm the married, monogamous type. I thought Anya was, too. Thank you for telling me. I need some time alone now."

"Sure." Impetuously Lydia leaned over and gave her aunt a quick hug, and then hurried out of the kitchen and out to her guesthouse, thinking how people got so danged nuts about sex. Like that stupid oversized dinner invitation from Luis that she had so carefully ignored. One drunken night of sex she couldn't remember and the boy thought they had a relationship?

No. Her situation was nothing like the moms'. Nothing at all.

19

This was hard. Really, really hard.

Kiley lay on a chaise lounge near the family pool at the country club, a copy of *Rolling Stone* open in her lap though she hadn't read a word. Over at the adult pool, scuba class was under way. Bruce, Jerry, Sedah, and all the others were doing underwater work with Roger cheerleading and teaching. Meanwhile, she was here alone watching Sid, Serenity, Jimmy, and Martina take part in a kids' swim meet.

"Time to eat, sweet pea," Lydia trilled. "We're talking major feast."

The club was jammed on this hot, sunny summer afternoon, and the poolside waiters were insanely busy, so Lydia had made a run to the club restaurant and had just returned carrying a tray fit for a four-star restaurant. This was no real surprise, since the club had recently hired away Le Bernardin's sous chef to take over its kitchen. To say the change in the kitchen was a popular move was an understatement. Since the arrival of Jean-François, membership applications had jumped by five hundred percent. There was now a seven-year waiting list, even assuming you could get the unanimous approval that the committee bylaws required.

Kiley looked up at Lydia dully. "What?"

"Eat," Lydia repeated. "We've got raw oysters—purported to be quite the aphrodisiac, although the Amas had better stuff—pan-roasted squab for two, asparagus hollandaise, and mesclun salad. I have no idea what mesclun is but it came highly recommended. You know, signing privileges here is one of the great advantages of my life."

"No thanks."

"Aw, come on. I even got you a Vernor's soda," Lydia cajoled. "It looks like carbonated piss but I know you love the stuff."

Kiley shrugged. "I'm not hungry."

"Or I can go back and get you a burger, fries, and a shake. They still offer that stuff on the kids' menu."

Kiley just sat there, so Lydia set down the tray anyway.

"You're turning down food from a girl who dined on monkey. Food has deep meaning to me."

"Sorry." She swung her legs around, using her hand to block the brilliant sun. "Is Esme here yet?"

Lydia scooped up an oyster, tilted her head back, and slurped it into her mouth and down her throat. "Not bad. Anyway, Esme said she'd be here by one. She and Tarshea have the afternoon free. She's been prepping Tarshea for her interview with Ann Marie. I think it's tomorrow."

You go to that good university out there and see someone who specializes in this, Kiley.

"Kiley!"

"Yeah?"

"We're gonna figure out a way for you to beat this thing, you know. Don't you worry."

Kiley nodded without enthusiasm. She'd told Lydia all about her problems in scuba class, and even talking about it was physically painful. Lydia, though, was the kind of person who never looked on the dark side. No matter how bleak the problem, Lydia believed that the application of a great brain, finesse, and prodigious imagination could set anything right.

Lydia dropped another raw oyster down her throat. "Damn. Beats peacock bass sushi any day of the week. Did you know that in Texas folks eat something called prairie oysters, which are actually bull testicles?"

Kiley laughed in spite of herself. "What does that have to do with anything?"

"Very little, but it did lighten the mood, chickadee. Now, eat some of the squab before I put some on my fork and play here-comes-the-blow-dart."

Again, Kiley laughed. Then she forked up a piece of the squab and chewed. "It's good."

"Good? Good? It's orgasmic. Well, almost."

"Your mind is a very scary place." Kiley swung her legs around to keep half an eye on Serenity and Sid. Both of them were standing by the side of the pool with their friends, waiting to be called for their events. Martina looked quite a bit slimmer, Kiley noted. She hoped the girl wasn't dieting.

179

"Look on the bright side. You'll never die of the bends." Lydia wagged an impaled morsel of squab at Kiley. "And don't you go givin' me that evil eye of yours, either. You have to try."

Kiley knew Lydia was right. But it was damn hard. The night before when she'd been unable to sleep, she'd surfed the Internet and researched panic disorders because she hadn't done any looking at the subject since junior high school. There'd actually been a fair amount of new research. Some of it was encouraging, and some of it was depressing as hell.

Onset—there were always exceptions, of course—was commonly between the ages of eighteen and twenty-four.

Gee, lucky me, Kiley had thought glumly. *My onset was a year early.*

More women got it than men. Doctors were prescribing Paxil and Zoloft to help sufferers and were getting decent results if the cases weren't too severe. Psychotherapy was an option, too. There was also something called aversion therapy, where you tried to do whatever it was that panicked you while under the supervision of a trained therapist.

As she pushed the expensive food around on her plate, Kiley told Lydia everything she'd learned.

"You know, panic is not unknown in the Amazon basin. I'm telling you, a short guy with his penis tied to his belly and a spear in his hand who gets into a tizzy can be a mite dangerous. Here. Drink this." Lydia popped open the can of Vernor's and handed it to Kiley.

"I bet." Kiley took the soda.

"It's not like we could run to the nearest drugstore for a prescription. But there are some herbal things that can really chill a person out that I bet your mother never tried."

180

Kiley could only imagine. She'd once seen Lydia temporarily paralyze a guy with some of her herbs. But she wasn't about to resort to ingesting unknown substances from Amazonia. At least not yet.

"How about if I tell you something that's really worth panicking over?" Lydia asked as she polished off the squab. "Anya's cheating on my aunt."

Kiley nearly dropped her soda. "You're kidding. How do you know?"

"Heard her having phone sex. That woman knows a thing or two."

"Okay. First of all, eww. Second of all, are you sure the moms don't have an open . . . whatever you'd call it? Marriage?"

Lydia shook her head. "I told my aunt. I could tell she was flipped out to hear that Anya is a big ol' ho."

"Hey, don't be so harsh. Maybe Anya just made a mistake. Like you did," Kiley added pointedly.

"Please," Lydia scoffed. "Am I on the phone with Luis talkin' about what I want to do with him and in what position behind Billy's back?"

"I don't know. Are you?"

"All day, every day." Lydia's tone was sour.

"Joking," Kiley assured her. "I feel bad for your aunt. Who do you think it is?"

"No clue, which is what I told Kat." Lydia wiped her hands on the scarlet linen napkin, and then reached into her Michael Kors toffee leather satchel for her sunglasses.

Kiley frowned. "Is that bag new?"

"Yep. Kat gave it to me. Well, she loaned it to me and never asked for it back. Where was I? Oh yeah, Anya's 'friend.' " She put on her sunglasses. "Anya travels in that whole Hollywood jock-gay-mafia thing. Those women aren't afraid to play musical beds."

Kiley made a face. "How do you know?"

"Kiley, open your eyes. Don't you see who's hanging with whom over at the adult pool? You gonna finish your squab?"

Kiley pushed her plate toward Lydia. "Maybe it's Evelyn Bowers. I hear she's available."

Lydia guffawed. "Now see, your life cannot be utter misery if you're still making jokes." She glanced over at the swim meet, and then toward the far end of the pool. "Check it out: Here comes the third musketeer. And she's not alone."

Kiley turned to see Esme heading toward them. She was definitely not alone. Jorge was with her. He wore black jeans and a navy T-shirt, and carried a small black backpack.

"Welcome to the club, Jorge!" Lydia called.

"I invited Jorge as my guest, since I don't have the kids until later," Esme explained when she reached them. She was dressed simply, in long black shorts and a long-sleeved white T-shirt.

"Where's Tarshea?" asked Lydia.

"In the club salon. Diane's paid for a manicure/pedicure for her before her interview. I offered one to Jorge," she joked, "but he refused."

"And miss this show? I wanted to see how the other half lives," Jorge joked. "Okay, now I've seen it."

Sugar on a shingle, Kiley thought, which was something her mom would say when someone broke a dish at the Derby. Kiley had resolved to talk to Jorge, to tell him that she'd had a chance to give it a lot of thought and that her heart was telling

182

her they shouldn't go any further than being friends. She didn't buy Lydia's theory about having Jorge as an FBG, either. Having had her panic attack was liberating, in a way. She was sure she wanted Tom. She didn't know for sure if Tom wanted her. But if he didn't want her, she wasn't going to settle.

Kiley knew that Esme would easily handle a talk like this. Lydia could do it in her sleep—she might even make up some lie to make the whole thing go easier. But Kiley had very little experience when it came to boys. Plus, she really liked Jorge. He had been nothing but wonderful to her, especially during those first terrible days after Platinum's arrest, when Kiley had lived at his parents' bungalow in Echo Park. The thought of hurting him filled her with dread.

"How are you, Kiley?" he asked.

"Okay."

God, this was awkward.

He smiled as if they were part of a secret society of two. "Can we talk?"

"Umm . . . sure."

"Alone?"

Damn. He was going to ask her out again, she was sure of it.

"Sure," she said again, realizing that she sounded stupider than a stupid girl, and she loathed stupid girls.

"Great. Why don't you show me around? It's my first time here and I want the whole corrupt experience."

Kiley excused herself, and started Jorge on a shortened version of the Brentwood Hills Country Club grand tour. The restaurants, arts and crafts center, playroom, locker rooms, grass and clay tennis courts, eighteen-hole golf facilities with driving range and putting course, shuffleboard courts, adult game room for cards and billiards, day spa—they saw blissful Tarshea under the meticulous care of a rotund manicurist—meeting rooms, and lush green gardens designed and personally planted by Patrick Chasse, the first curator of landscape at the Gardner Museum in Boston. Kiley mostly talked, and Jorge mostly listened. But try as she might for an opening to broach the subject of their future relationship, or lack thereof, the topic never came up.

He broached it for her, as they stepped out of the breezeway between the pools. "Hold up a minute. We need to talk before we go back. About us."

Double damn.

"Okay."

"That night at the Conga Room . . . kissing you . . . it was nice."

She nodded, but couldn't find her voice. It had been nice. And she was attracted to him. How could she explain that she didn't want to lose his friendship, that—

"But I think we should just be friends."

Kiley blinked. What did he just say?

"This isn't easy for me. I have a lot of respect for you, Kiley. You're smart, and you're beautiful, and you've got a lot of guts. Not many girls from Minnesota—"

"Wisconsin," she corrected, very aware of his arm still around her.

"Sorry, Wisconsin—would come to California like you did, and stay here by themselves because they're determined to go to Scripps. The way you love the ocean . . . it's like a passion for you. I know what that feels like."

Ha. If he only knew.

"But here's the thing," he went on. "Esme is my best friend. And she's one of your best friends. And the whole thing . . . it feels complicated, you know? Like maybe Esme could be stuck in the middle."

Kiley wasn't sure she followed this logic. Unless . . .

"Do you . . . want to be with Esme?"

Jorge moved his arm. "Nah."

Kiley studied him. He denied it, but the truth was written on his face. "She's a wonderful girl, Jorge."

"I know that. And I know all about her and Jonathan, just like I knew all about her and Junior. That's just Esme doing what Esme always does. Smart girl, bad judgment."

"Okay."

"Anyway, are we good, Kiley?" Jorge's eyes searched her. She could see that he was as concerned about hurting her or losing her friendship as she had been about him.

"We're good," she assured him.

As they shared a warm hug, she mused on how life was just so ironic. He loved Esme, and she loved the ocean. Why did it happen so often that people loved the one thing they couldn't have?

20

Tarshea looked dubiously at the steering wheel. "I don't think I should be drivin', Lydia."

"Aw, come on," Lydia urged. "You only die once. Live a little dangerously!"

"But I've never driven anything before."

Lydia patted Tarshea's slender arm. "Tarshea, sweet pea. Take a deep breath. It's just a harmless little ol' golf cart."

It was an hour later. The girls had arrived after their stint with the psychologist, and Esme had taken them to the activities center in the main clubhouse to watch *Dora the Explorer*. It was still their favorite show. Kiley was still up at the pool with Jorge. Lydia wasn't sure what was going on with them but made a mental note to call Kiley later and find out.

When Tarshea expressed an interest in seeing the golf course,

Lydia volunteered to take her down, not even caring if she ran into Luis. They'd gone through the clubhouse, toured the practice range, and finished up at the double line of golf carts by the clubhouse. Rich people, Lydia had explained to Tarshea, did not walk the course unless they were fitness fanatics.

Lydia eyed the carts and thought how much fun it would be to drive one. She missed that piece-of-crap car that Luis had loaned her. Now that she was car-less, even a golf cart looked good to her.

Once Lydia got an idea in her head, she was like a harpy eagle that had just dug its claws into a lame monkey—she just couldn't let go. So she excused herself to go chat up a clubhouse attendant, threw in some serious flirting, and got his permission to take one of the golf carts out for a jaunt around the course. It would be a three-and-a-half-mile scenic drive if they stayed on the designated paths.

"I thought you wanted to drive," Tarshea reminded Lydia.

"I do. I'll drive next time. Your turn."

Tarshea blew out a long breath and plucked nervously at the hem of the scoop-neck T-shirt that Esme had evidently loaned her. Lydia thought that Esme filled it out better, but Tarshea had such an elegant line to her body that she looked great in pretty much anything.

"Okay. Wheel to turn, pedal on the right for forward, pedal on the left for the stopping," Tarshea murmured. "What else? How do I go in reverse?"

Lydia pointed to a red knob on the console between them. "Flip that to the other side."

Tarshea started the golf cart's electric engine and then

pulled the knob. But she must not have moved it far enough, because when she put her foot on the accelerator, the cart slammed forward. *Wham!* They smacked the rear end of another cart.

"That's it!" Tarshea pushed the brake to the floor and hopped out. "I'm not driving anymore."

"Come on, Tarshea." Lydia patted the white upholstered driver's seat. "You can't give up over one teeny tiny setback."

Tarshea shook her head. "You got the wrong girl. I'm not driving that thing."

For a moment, Lydia considered pressing the issue. She remembered the first time in Amazonia that she'd been permitted to paddle a dugout canoe on her own on the Rio Negro. Unknown to everyone—how could they know, since there wasn't anything resembling a local weather report on their hand-cranked shortwave radio?—violent thunderstorms fifty miles upstream had dumped seven inches of rain into the river. She'd been paddling out toward the center when the water flow suddenly swept her downstream. Her ten-year-old arms were helpless against it, her shouts for help unheard.

She managed to beach the dugout three miles downstream of their hamlet, and spent an anxious afternoon alone on the riverbank waiting for help to arrive. Finally, two Ama tribesmen on a monkey hunt spotted her. When the trio hiked back to the village, the Amas insisted that Lydia's parents put her right back in another dugout canoe. From the Ama point of view, the only way to conquer fear was to confront it. Her parents had agreed with the tribesmen.

She'd screamed bloody murder and felt betrayed by her own parents, who she was sure wanted her to die.

Afterward, Lydia was glad. She'd thought about sharing the Ama philosophy with Kiley, but had decided to bide her time.

"Tell you what." Lydia edged over to the driver's position. "I'll start us out, you can watch me, and then you can take over. How about that?"

Tarshea slid into the passenger seat, eyeing Lydia warily. "How many times have you driven one of these?"

"None." Lydia pushed the red lever firmly into the Reverse position. "Here we go."

The cart proved easy to maneuver. They backed out of the parking space, and Lydia saw that there was fortunately no damage to the rear end of the cart that Tarshea had smacked. Then she shifted the red lever and put her foot on the accelerator. The cart eased forward under her guidance. Dang. This was simple.

"You make it look easy," Tarshea said. "And I appreciate the tour you gave me, too."

"Why, thank you. Compliments will get you everywhere." Lydia saw the sign leading to the first tee, and turned the cart in that direction. "Dang, driving this puppy really is fun. Of course, I'd rather have a Lamborghini."

Tarshea grinned. "Cherry red, with black leather seats."

"Oh yeah," Lydia agreed. "You are my kind of girl."

"Until I came to America, the only Lamborghini I ever saw was on the television. What amazes me is, in America, if you want to become rich, you have the chance to become rich. Isn't that true?"

189

"I suppose it is," Lydia agreed. "Public school is free. And if you get high grades you can get a scholarship to college. And then . . . well, I guess you can be whatever you want to be."

"Amazing. In Jamaica there is no opportunity. You and I, we both want to be rich. But Kiley doesn't care about money, am I right?"

"She will if she can't afford to get into Scripps. That's the college she wants to attend." The cart passed under a canopy of leafy trees.

"You and Kiley and Esme, you are all so different from each other," Tarshea mused as Lydia piloted the cart smoothly along. "Back home, most of my friends were all like me. Poor girls with not much future."

"It's the nanny thing that brought us together. When you're a nanny too, you'll see how it's like . . . well, a common denominator, I guess." They passed a foursome on the first fairway waiting for another foursome to clear the number one green before they hit their approach shots. "Kind of us against the world. You'll be a nanny soon. Which means you'll be one of us. Did you see the butt on that guy waiting to hit?"

Tarshea gave Lydia a mischievous look. "Yeah. But so far I haven't done much more than a lot of looking."

"Oh, I used to be like that, too," Lydia said airily. "You'll see that here in la-la land, temptation is everywhere. It's a beautiful thing." They passed the first green and headed over a wooden footbridge that led to the second hole. "Check out what's in the cooler in the back, okay?"

Tarshea turned around and opened the red cooler just

behind them. She reported that it was full of ice and stocked with Corona and Rolling Rock beer, wine spritzers, bottled water, juice, and sandwiches of various types wrapped in plastic.

"I'll take a Corona," Lydia told her.

Tarshea twisted back around. "All of that must be for club guests! And you aren't twenty-one!"

"Tarshea, Tarshea, Tarshea." Lydia patted her knee and continued to drive forward. "You've got a lot to learn about the lifestyles of the rich and famous. Of which you are now a part." She slowed the cart, reached back, and nabbed a Corona.

"I have a feeling you grew up a rich girl, and that's why you're so at home with all of this."

Lydia laughed so hard she practically spilled her beer.

"What's so funny?"

"It's an epic."

As they continued their scenic tour of the golf course, Lydia found herself telling Tarshea the whole story of how it was that she'd come to be Kat and Anya's nanny, with many choice details of her life in Amazonia. Tarshea was a wonderful and active listener, asking probing questions that were all about Lydia and not at all about herself. Her ingenuousness was charming.

Somewhere between the eighth and ninth holes, Lydia pulled off the asphalt and onto the grass. "Your turn," she told Tarshea. "You drive."

"No way. Next time."

Lydia wagged a finger at her. "Your new life is gonna be chock-full of adventures. You need to just wade on in, Tarshea. You can't be a wuss and have any fun at all."

"Me? A 'wuss'?"

Lydia nodded and took a long pull on her beer. Tarshea gave her a determined look.

"Never a wuss, mon. I'm driving."

Lydia hooted and switched places with Tarshea. "Now that's what I'm talkin' about!"

There were a few jerks and stops as Tarshea figured out how much pressure to put on the accelerator and brakes, but soon she was handling the golf cart like a pro. They reached the eleventh hole, and waited for a threesome on the tee to hit before cruising past them. Lydia was psyched when Tarshea kept her speed up once they got going again. There were two golfers walking on the fairway ahead, hand in hand; their clubs were slung over their shoulders.

Tarshea pointed to the couple. "That's so sweet."

Lydia saw the tall gentleman let go of his partner so that his right hand could make a discreet journey to her buff, shorts-clad ass. The gesture made Lydia think of Billy. She wondered if he'd ever had sex on a golf course. They'd have to do it late at night when the course was empty, but she saw no reason why she couldn't make it soon. Maybe right here, in fact.

Tarshea continued up the fairway, and Lydia snuck a look back at the couple. The guy's hand was still on her—

Holy shit. It couldn't be. Could it? Yep. No doubt.

"Fuck a duck!" she exclaimed.

"Okay, my mudda just had a heart attack at your language—what's wrong?" Tarshea demanded.

"Uh . . . I thought I saw a rabbit about to jump in front of the cart," Lydia invented.

Suddenly, it all made sense. The phone sex. The *Kama Sutra* book Lydia had found in the moms' closet. It hadn't belonged to Aunt Kat at all. It had belonged to Anya, whom Lydia had been sure was a by-genetic-imprint lesbian. Nope. The loving couple that had been hand in hand, and then hand on ass, was Anya and the colonel.

21

"You stink!" Easton kicked Weston under the breakfast table, and Weston started howling.

"¡Paren ustedes ahora mismo!" Esme snapped. *Both of you stop that right now.* She wasn't even aware that she'd chastised them in Spanish until the words were out of her mouth. Weston had stopped crying instantly and both girls were staring at her with huge, luminous eyes.

Esme took a deep breath, and then spoke in a soft but authoritative tone. She hated yelling at the girls. "We still have to get you both dressed and ready for your mama. She is taking you someplace very wonderful and fun. Finish up so that we can get ready."

"No this," Easton said, pointing to the offending bowl of cereal in front of her. "Egg with hat."

"Egg with hat." Weston agreed.

Egg with hat. Thank God that phase was going to end soon

enough. Tarshea had her interview with Ann Marie this morning, and Esme prayed she'd get the job. She'd just about had it with Tarshea unwittingly showing her up at every turn. She got up earlier, found more fun things for the girls to do, was creative and artistic and smart and endlessly cheerful. On top of that, Tarshea's Spanish was improving on a daily basis. Time and again Esme would come upon the little girls snuggled up to Tarshea, who'd be reading *Olivia* or *The Cat in the Hat* to them. The twins didn't mind; they seemed to revel in the fact that they had two nannies.

Diane seemed to like it, too. Just that morning, she'd told Esme that Tarshea was setting a good example of how a nanny should be. She and Steven would be rewarding Tarshea for her volunteer efforts by taking her to the opening of Martin Scorsese's new film next week at the ArcLight.

Great, Esme had thought. *My own boss is telling me I need to shape up, and my boyfriend doesn't return my calls. Life is grand.*

Jonathan was still missing in action. The night she'd done Beverly's tattoo, she'd driven to his apartment. He hadn't been home. Some insanity made her wait an hour to see if he'd arrive. And if so, with whom. She finally gave up at three in the morning, and left a message on his cell: *Call me when you get in.* He hadn't.

"I done, Esme," Easton announced, showing Esme her empty cereal bowl.

"I done, too," Weston agreed.

"I'm done," Esme corrected. "Good girls." Esme checked her watch. In about a half hour, Diane would be taking the twins to a children's tea party at the Greystone Estate on Loma Vista Drive to benefit the International Children's Museum.

Esme still had to help the girls brush their teeth and hair, and dress them in their two-hundred-dollar cotton ruffled pinafores from Auntie Barbara's Antiques on Beverly Drive— pink for Easton, yellow for Weston—new white tights that would stay that color for approximately fifteen minutes, and black patent leather Mary Jane shoes.

As the girls pushed back from the table, Tarshea came running in.

"Hi, hi, so sorry it took so long. *Cómo están las dos princesas hermosas hoy?*" How are the two beautiful princesses today?

"*Bueno,*" Easton said, and both girls giggled.

"Try not to speak to them in Spanish," Esme said, carrying the cereal bowls to the dishwasher. "If you speak Spanish, they speak Spanish. How'd it go?"

Tarshea had worn a new black BCBG suit—courtesy of Diane's personal shopper—to the interview. Esme saw how well it suited her long, slender body. "Well, I'm not sure. Ann Marie wasn't there."

"What?"

"Her secretary interviewed me. Is that how people do it in America?"

As Esme and Tarshea got the girls upstairs and into their party outfits, Tarshea explained that she and this secretary had sat in a lavender den. She had neither met the children nor gone on a tour of the house. The assistant had said her job was just to get a feel for Tarshea and the other candidates. She would be recommending the two finalists for the nanny job to her boss. Only then would Ann Marie interview the applicants.

"Is that the way it is usually done in America?" Tarshea queried again.

Esme wrestled to stuff Easton's wriggling right foot into one black Mary Jane. No luck. Easton kicked it into the far corner of her room.

"I don't know. Sometimes, I guess. Did she say when you would know if you were a finalist?"

"No problem, I've got it." Tarshea sang out her trademark Jamaican phrase and then trotted over to retrieve the shoe. She handed it to Esme, who reprimanded Easton, then held the girl's ankle firmly enough to stuff her foot into the Mary Jane.

"Well, did she tell you anything?" Esme pressed. "About when you'd know?"

Tarshea shook her head, bit her lip, and turned her sorrowful eyes to Esme. "I know you want your privacy again, Esme. You have done much too much for me already. If I don't get this position, I will find another one with Steven and Diane's help. They promise me."

"No, no, don't worry about it," Esme found herself saying.

She handed Tarshea a brush, and they both went to work on the little girls' hair. Why was it, Esme wondered, that whenever she had a conversation with Tarshea, she ended up apologizing?

After Diane and the girls departed, Esme went back to the guesthouse, while Tarshea worked out in the Goldhagens' home gym. Diane had encouraged Esme to make use of the gym in her free time, but Esme had never set foot in the place. For one thing, the whole idea of exercising on machines struck

Esme as absurd. Her parents toiled twelve hours a day some-times, doing physical labor. People who came from that didn't need a gym.

Instead, she sat on the swing under the orange trees and ru-minated. Jonathan had still not called. What could it possibly mean? He hadn't come home at all? He'd come home but he'd been with that bitch Mackenzie? Either way, he would still pick up the phone messages on his cell. He was an actor, for God's sake. They always picked up their messages.

She went inside for a glass of water and found the kitchen sink dripping again—*drip, drip, drip.* Well, it gave her an ex-cuse to do something. Her father had taught her to be a prac-tical girl, so she thought nothing of getting the tool kit out from underneath the sink and going to work on the faucet. She unscrewed the handle, the sink bumping up against the hip pocket that held her cell phone. The one that refused to ring.

Suddenly, she knew whom she had to call. Not Lydia. Not Kiley. And definitely not Jonathan.

Jorge. He was the best listener in the world. Plus, he under-stood Esme and the world she came from, because it was his world, too. She still wondered what he and Kiley had talked about at the club when they'd gone off together. They'd both been quiet and even a little distant when they returned.

Esme quickly replaced the cracked washer, then got out her cell and pressed in Jorge's number.

"*Hola,*" he answered.

"It's me."

"What's up, me?" Jorge asked easily.

"Too much." With just a few polite preliminaries, she

quickly relayed the highlights of the Jonathan situation and how insane it was making her.

"Well, what do you want to do?" Jorge asked.

She stowed the toolbox back under the sink and wiped up the mess she'd made. "I want Jonathan to call me."

Her friend laughed. "I asked what you want to do, not what you want him to do. You can't control what he does."

Right. True.

"I want . . . I want to not care this much," she admitted, leaning against the refrigerator. "And I want to know exactly what's going on." She glanced at her watch. It was nearly eleven. Jonathan was shooting again today, at the same location in Topanga Canyon. "I want to go to the movie set and confront his ass," she added.

From the other end of the phone, all she got was silence.

"Jorge?"

"No one is stopping you, *esa*."

Esme closed her eyes. "I'm stopping me."

"Ah."

"Don't 'ah' me, Jorge," Esme said crossly. "Don't pull that enlightened shit with me."

He chuckled. "So don't pull your tough-barrio-chica shit with me then. Hey, the Latin Kings are playing tonight in the old neighborhood. You want to come back and forget your troubles?"

"I have to see if Diane needs me."

"Well, do what you got to do."

Esme thanked him and hung up, feeling no better. Why couldn't she simply take her mother's advice and fall for Jorge?

But no, she had to choose ex–gang leaders and rich gringo actors, guys guaranteed to mess with her mind and screw up her life.

She shed her clothes and headed for the shower. She would not call Jonathan. She would be more on the ball with the kids so that Diane would have faith in her again. She'd take the glitterati who wanted her tattoos for every penny she could get.

She was in charge.

22

"Oh, you are not wearing that," Platinum decreed when Kiley walked into the living room of the main house. Platinum had been moved up a level in her pretrial detention program, which meant that she was now allowed a weekly supervised visit to her estate to pick up clothes and see her children, always under the watchful eye of Ms. Johnson. Her actual trial was set for early September—she faced three to five years in prison if she was convicted on all the charges.

Ms. Johnson had called the colonel the night before to say that she'd be visiting tonight. But the colonel had already planned to take the kids to the MCAS Miramar Air Show in San Diego and refused to change his schedule. The good news was that they'd be home by ten, and he was never late. The bad news was that no one but Kiley was there to greet Platinum and the social worker.

As it turned out, Platinum was in better shape than Kiley

had anticipated. While Ms. Johnson retired to the kitchen to drink coffee and write up some reports, the rock star took the opportunity to bond with her nanny as if they were long-lost friends. The first few weeks of pretrial custody had been a bitch, though, she confessed. Withdrawal from drugs and alcohol didn't get any easier when you got older.

Of course, she was smoking like a fiend, and her language hadn't improved any, but she was clear-eyed and sober. Her perfect waterfall of platinum white hair fell nearly to her waist. She wore skinny white Seven jeans with pearl and crystal embroidery around the waist, and a sheer white Escada linen shirt with a crystal tie at the neckline left unknotted, so that the shirt fell off one shoulder. Underneath was a white Chloé pleated bra top. She looked absolutely perfect. It was hard to ignore the fashion advice of someone who looked absolutely perfect, even if it was Platinum.

"I thought casual would be good," Kiley explained.

"I hope you don't have a date."

"Actually, I do."

This was true. She and Tom had finally connected. He was picking her up at nine, after he finished shooting a commercial for a start-up jeans company that was paying him an obscene amount of money.

"With the model? Tom whatever-his-name-is?"

Kiley nodded.

"Jesus, Kiley. That jeans-and-a-T-shirt thing screams *high school*. When you get dressed you have to look in the mirror and ask: Would I do me? Let that be your guide."

"Honestly, Platinum, I'm not very good at this stuff."

"Big shocker there." Platinum sucked her unfiltered Camel deeply, and exhaled a ragged smoke ring. "Come with me."

Kiley only had a little while before Tom was supposed to pick her up, but Platinum was already ascending the staircase to the second floor, so Kiley trotted after her. The rock star went straight to her own white-on-white suite and the adjoining bedroom she'd transformed into a massive walk-in closet.

One entire side was devoted to white clothes, the other to prints and solids. Kiley watched, amazed, as Platinum marched back and forth between the racks, scrutinizing her choices the way the colonel scrutinized the kids when he gave them a lecture. Finally she stopped abruptly.

"This," she decreed, and pulled a gossamer top of palest peach off its matching peach velvet hanger.

"Oh no," Kiley declared. "I mean, I still have that beautiful shirt you gave me and I just—I can't take another one."

"What shirt?"

"In my guesthouse? You took off one that you were wearing and gave it to me? I was going to a party with Tom?"

"I don't remember," Platinum admitted. "But do yourself a favor and take this."

Kiley took it. It was simple and elegant, with bell-shaped sleeves and tiny rhinestone buttons. "It's beautiful."

"It should be, it's Yves Saint goddamn Laurent. It'll fit you, too, because it's meant to be drapey. And take this, and this, and this." She began pulling various shirts from their hangers and flinging them in Kiley's direction.

"Platinum—no—I mean, I can't—"

"Okay, you so need to shut up," Platinum said, tossing

Kiley a pair of white trousers. "Try these Betsey Johnson pants—they stretch."

"Why are you doing this?" Kiley asked. Platinum was hardly known for her generosity.

"Because, Kiley, you're as crazy as I am."

"I am not!"

"Oh, come on. My brother-in-law is a Nazi. How can you stand him? Any sane nanny would have gone to the breezeway at the club and gotten poached. Well, don't just stand there. Take off that ugly-ass crap you're wearing and try some real clothes on."

They went back into Platinum's bedroom, where Kiley changed. Off came the jeans and T-shirt, on went the pale peach shirt. It fit marvelously, skimming over her curves. Then she added the white pants. She'd been certain that her butt would approximate the size and color of the Abominable Snowman, but the pants were so well made that they looked great.

"Great ass," Platinum commented offhandedly as she lit another Camel. "Not that anyone would know in that baggy shit you wear."

Kiley wasn't sure "thanks" was an appropriate response, so she gestured to the huge pile of clothes on the bed. "This is so nice of you, Platinum."

"Oh please, I am not nice, and I am not suddenly going to become nice. You're my goddamn Berlin Wall here, Kiley. You are all that stands between my children and that bastard my sister married. Consider the clothes a bribe. There's more where they came from."

Kiley's cell phone sounded; she had to scramble for her just-removed jeans to answer. "Hello?"

"Hey, it's me, Lydia. You have a minute? There's something I need to talk to you about."

"Can it wait? I've got a date with Tom. In ten minutes."

"For Tom it definitely can wait. It's important, but don't try to call me back. Billy and I are going to be occupied this evening. How about you?"

By her use of the word "occupied," Lydia left little doubt as to the activity that was planned.

"Don't know. I'll have to see."

"Give me the blow-by-blow," Lydia advised. "I'll call you tomorrow."

As her friend was saying goodbye, Tom clicked in. "I'm outside the gate. Can you open it?"

"Come on up. I'll meet you in front of the main house. Five minutes."

"Leave the clothes," Platinum instructed when Kiley hung up. "I'll get one of the maids to put them in the guesthouse."

"Thank you so—"

Platinum held up a palm of silence. "Got it. You're pathetically grateful. Now go meet your guy."

Then, Platinum did the most startling thing Kiley had ever seen her do. She smiled.

Tom suggested a new casual restaurant on the Venice Beach boardwalk called the Seafarer. They sat at an outdoor redwood table and basked in the warm glow of the standing heating poles that graced so many of Los Angeles's outdoor establishments. The boardwalk, famous for its street performers and eccentrics, was close to deserted at ten o'clock at night.

They'd both ordered the house specialty, fish and chips, and an amazing fruit drink made from pureed peaches, pineapple, papaya, and coconut. The conversation was low-key— his modeling gig, her latest misadventures with the colonel, and the brief return of Platinum to her estate. It was all very newsy and casual, like good friends catching up. Actually, like casual friends catching up, Kiley mentally amended. Casual friends to whom you don't tell the important stuff.

But how could Kiley share the weight of depression she felt, about how her goals that used to be elusive but were still possible, were now utterly impossible? If she found the attacks unattractive in her own mother, what would Tom think of them? She didn't want to find out. Not that it mattered. Nothing he had said or done since picking her up at Platinum's had led Kiley to think that Tom wanted anything more than buddy-buddy friendship.

Just when the ineffable sadness of that notion was hitting her, Tom reached across the table and touched her hand. "So here's my question, Kiley McCann. How did things get weird between us?"

Her heart skipped a beat. Maybe not so buddy-buddy after all, then.

Thank you, God.

He sat there in the glow of the heat lamp, the subdued outdoor lighting glinting off his golden hair, looking more delectable than any human had the right to look. He wore a T-shirt the same blue as his eyes, casually loose jeans, and Bass Weejuns.

Though Kiley was sporting Platinum's beautiful shirt and sexy pants, she knew what passersby must have been thinking: What the hell does that gorgeous guy see in her? She felt it whenever they were together. There had always been girls trying to catch Tom's eye. But how did you tell a guy any of that without seeming insecure and pathetic? You didn't. However insecure and pathetic she felt in Tom's presence, opening up about it would up the awful quotient exponentially.

"Well . . . I thought maybe you wanted us to just be friends."

He looked perplexed. "Why?"

"You're so busy."

"I'm busy?" he echoed, sounding confused. "What does that have to do with anything?"

"I barely heard from you when you were in Florida."

"Jeez, Kiley. That's what this is about?"

She flushed. "Yes."

He shook his head. "Then you're rewriting history, which is not such an admirable trait. The last time we talked before I went to Florida, I was dropping you at Platinum's place. You were pissed at me because I hadn't called you 'my girlfriend' when I introduced you to some friends at Cafe Med. You told me we'd talk later. I thought, fine, let her think this through. She'll call me. And now, you're pissed I didn't call you? Kiley, the ball was in your court. I was waiting for *you*."

The waitress brought their fish and chips, which gave Kiley a moment to think. Tom was right about the time line, that was true. So she apologized.

"What's really going on here, Kiley?" he pressed.

She chewed thoughtfully on a single french fry. Then, to

her surprise, she heard her mother's words again, as if on the breeze.

Kiley McCann. I did not raise my daughter to be a liar and we have been down this road before. I warn you, do not lie to me. It's you, isn't it?

It was her. At least as much as him.

"Tom, I spend my days with little kids. You spend yours with the most beautiful women in the world. I can't compete."

Tom looked incredulous. "That's what this is about?"

She nodded and reached for her fruit drink just to have something to do. At the next table, two high school girls tittered, glancing at them and then quickly looking away. Kiley was sure they recognized Tom from either his recent role in *The Ten* or his billboards.

"Kiley, if I wanted to be with a model, I'd be with a model. Do you really not know how attracted I am to you?"

She could feel her cheeks burn. "I . . . uh . . ."

He put his knuckles to her cheek; his eyes exuded so much heat that Kiley thought she would simply melt and slide under the table. Then he pulled some bills from his wallet and threw them onto the table. "We need to get out of here."

They walked across the boardwalk—actually just a wide strip of gray asphalt—and then they were on the broad beach. The closer they got to the water, the quieter it became, save for the insistent calling of some nighttime terns that picked at the edible detritus of the day's sun worshippers.

"These girls I work with—the ones you think are so beautiful," Tom began, his voice low. "Most of them are completely self-centered. It's like the whole world exists just to be a reflection of their beauty."

"Hold on while I get a tissue. Poor them."

Tom smiled. "Okay, let me try again. Kiley. On my dog Blue's life . . ." He held up a hand as if taking an oath. "I simply am not attracted to bony women."

"What?"

His hand was still in the air.

"I am not attracted to tall, bony women," he repeated. "Never have been. Never will be."

Kiley laughed. "Now you're the one who's joking."

"Alisa, my first girlfriend in eighth grade? She was so round and cute, with the greatest red hair. She had a pet pig and wanted to be a vet. I was crazy for her. My high school girl-friend, Laurie? Five-foot-nothing and very curvy—definitely not skinny. She's at MIT now."

Kiley's head was spinning. "But—but Marym . . ."

"I know the world thinks Marym is the epitome of beauty," Tom acknowledged. "I like her because she's a truly nice person, regardless of the crap that went down between the two of you. She's smart as hell."

"Oh come on," Kiley scoffed.

"What kind of guys are you used to, Kiley? The kind that base who they're attracted to on what the world thinks? I've never been like that. And I can't believe you'd be into that kind of guy."

Kiley decided against admitting that her only real high school relationship had been based more on "well, he asked me out" than on any great chemistry.

"The girls I've really liked have had a lot in common," Tom went on. "They were all on the short side, none of 'em were skinny, and they were all passionately interested in something

209

besides navel-gazing. I mean, my concept of hell is to be stranded on a desert island with an airhead whose claim to fame is that she modeled in *Vogue*."

Kiley laughed. "Mine too, now that you mention it."

"I have this favorite book—my mom used to read it to me and my sister when we were kids—maybe you know it. *The Little Prince*."

Kiley nodded. "I know it. We read it in tenth-grade French."

"Well, it's about . . . about dreams, I guess. There's this line that always stays with me: 'What is essential is invisible to the eye.' "

A gust of wind blew some hair over Kiley's eyes and Tom tenderly brushed it away. "You are a beautiful girl, Kiley. On the outside, even if you don't know it. But what means more to me is the essential part on the inside. You're not jaded. You don't pretend to be. I love how much you love the ocean, how that fuels your hopes and dreams."

Kiley felt as if someone had slapped her cheek. Tom must have read it in her face.

"What?" he asked. "Did I say something wrong?"

She gulped hard.

"What? Tell me."

"The ocean . . ."

She looked out at the sea, instead of at him, as she let the whole story spill out. The aborted scuba diving lesson. Her panic attack. The history of it in her family; her grandmother, her mother.

"I guess that's the real me, invisible to the eye," she concluded, her voice hoarse.

Tom gathered her into his arms and held her. "Can I ask you something?"

Kiley nodded.

"What happened underwater—it never happened before. Right?"

"Yes."

"Has it happened since?"

"I haven't been in the pool."

Tom stepped back and rubbed his chin. "Do you think . . . what time do you start work in the morning?"

"I don't, actually. The colonel is taking the kids flying at Edwards Air Force Base. I don't need to be home until noon."

"What would you say if I picked you up around five a.m.?"

"Did you say five?"

Tom nodded. "There's someplace I'd like to take you."

Kiley couldn't think of anything open at five except the diner where her mother worked.

"Where?"

He looked at her with his clear blue eyes, the eyes that had vicariously seduced a million women and a whole lot of gay men. Eyes that now were looking at her and seeing only her. "Trust me, Kiley. I think you can do that."

23

"Now, this is the life I was meant to live." As Lydia stretched with languid pleasure, the two-thousand-dollar cinnabar vine-and-bamboo-patterned chinoiserie sheet fell from her naked breasts. "Sanity has been restored to the world."

Billy nuzzled her neck. "If you'd never left Texas, you'd be a much more boring girl, Lydia."

"I suppose that's true. But now that I have a greater appreciation for all things decadent, I say we make up for lost time. More Cristal and beluga sound about right? I'll call down to room service. And then . . . second helpings of you, too."

He kissed her quickly. "Hold that thought. Nature calls."

As he departed for the bathroom—which also held a marble tub, bidet, shower with four jets, and Jacuzzi tub—she admired the rear view, then propped herself up on three of the fluffy pillows and regarded this magnificent hotel penthouse suite with utter contentment.

The Beverly-Florence was Beverly Hills's newest boutique hotel. Located north of Sunset Boulevard just off Benedict Canyon, it held only twenty-five rooms and suites, each of them decorated by a different interior designer except for the renowned Harry Schnaper. He got to do two.

One of the remarkable features was that everything in every room was for sale. By the bedside, there was a price list along with the room service menu, like one would find in a New York City art gallery. Check off the appropriate items, let the charges be approved by American Express, and any and all of what you wanted for yourself would be delivered to your residence the next day, no matter whether it was Bergenfield, Brussels, or Beijing. This wasn't avarice on the part of the management. Instead, it was a service to their guests, because the furnishings were so exquisite.

Thanks to a friend of a friend of Billy's, they were in a three-room suite for the price of a double room at the Holiday Inn. The living room featured a Kendrake green cowhide circular couch ($42,999) in front of the wood-burning fireplace, plus a Giorgetti love seat ($4,999) and matching chairs ($2,500 each). Entertainment, should they want it, could be found on the sixty-inch Sony plasma television ($5,999).

An archway led to a thousand-square-foot bedroom with Spanish hand-carved mesquite furniture, plus a matching four-poster bed with a sheer red silk canopy ($87,000). There was a small fridge by the far wall that had been stocked with fresh fruit, various exotic cheeses, a one-pound tin of Russian beluga 000 caviar Malossol ($2,120) and a bottle of Cristal champagne ($300).

Lydia called down to room service for more caviar and

champagne; the authoritative voice at the other end said it would be up in thirty or forty minutes; they'd just had to ice the Cristal. Would that be satisfactory? They didn't want to be indiscreet with their delivery.

Nice. Discretion. What a concept. Such a far cry from what she'd seen on the golf course with Tarshea. Lydia still hadn't told her aunt, but knew she had to, and soon. Tonight the moms had given her the evening off. They were taking the children to visit some friends who lived in Huntington Beach. Family time for Kat with a cheating spouse. All Lydia had to do was be home by sunup.

Billy stepped back into the bedroom wearing a plush white terry cloth robe. "There's a rose-scented bubble bath in that bronze tub with our names on it. I'll answer the door for room service. Don't even think about getting out."

She padded into the bathroom and stepped into the bubble-filled tub, twice as deep and half again as long as a standard bathtub. The rose scent that wafted from the oiled water was heavenly. She laid her head back against the lip and closed her eyes.

She heard Billy phone down to the restaurant and ask to add a pint of the Beverly-Florence's own homemade vodka-cherry ice cream and one spoon. Lydia smiled. She wanted to ask him about whether he would be willing to spend some time with Jimmy—she couldn't think of a better role model. This, however, didn't seem the time or place for that particular query. It could wait.

She slid down to where bubbles tickled her chin. If the Amas found out about this, they'd all move to Los Angeles.

*　*　*

The suite door had a discreet chime instead of a knocker; they were both dozing in the tub when they heard it sound, and the shouted announcement that followed. "Room service!"

"I'll get it," Billy told her.

Lydia sat up. "I'm getting out too. Or else I'll turn into a prune."

"Coming!" Billy called as he helped her out of the tub and into another of the hotel's luxurious robes. They walked hand in hand to the door.

"Can you handle more?" Lydia asked coquettishly.

"Champagne? Or you?"

"Both."

"For a girl who was a virgin a few days ago, I appreciate your appetite," he quipped.

"Good to know I'm a quick study." Lydia didn't have the slightest pang of guilt about Billy's virgin remark. The experience with Luis had been entirely rationalized. She didn't remember what happened. If she didn't remember, she couldn't tell Billy.

He smiled into her eyes and smoothed some hair from her cheek. "Admit it. This was worth waiting for."

They opened the door.

It wasn't room service. It was Luis.

"Hi, Lydia," he said to her, offering her a white garment on a platter. "You forgot this at my house. I thought you might need it."

"What the hell are you doing here, man?" Billy was furious. "I'm calling hotel security!"

"No need, no need." Luis backed away from the door. "I just thought your lady might need her shirt. She never came back for it. I'm out of here." He took two steps toward the elevator, and then stopped. When he turned around, his eyes bored in on Lydia's. "You need better manners. When a gentleman sends you a special invitation to dine with him, manners require the courtesy of a response. Have a pleasant evening. I know from experience that you will, Billy. Very pleasant."

One time in the Amazon—she hadn't been there very long—Lydia had been walking down to the river to fish. She'd stepped over a fallen log without checking to see what was on the other side and came down on a young bushmaster snake, which promptly clamped its jaws against her bare ankle. As the deadly venom coursed into her, with the real possibility of death if she didn't get back to her father's medical attention immediately, she couldn't believe that she had been that stupid.

The same thing was happening now, only there was no Daddy-the-bush-doctor to run to for help. In fact, she wished there was a full-grown bushmaster—all thirteen or fourteen deadly feet of one—in the suite that would be willing to send her to the Great Beyond with its fangs right now.

Anything, even death, was better than the pain and betrayal on Billy Martin's face.

24

Everyone always talked about beautiful California sunsets, with the ocean as a backdrop and the ball of fire awash in pink clouds as it slid into the night. This was the first sunrise that Kiley had seen since she'd come to California, and she had to say that it rivaled any sunset. The sky blazed bright red in the east toward Palm Springs as she and Tom drove in his pickup on I-10, toward Pomona and San Bernardino. Los Angeles was still asleep; the calm quiet before the insanity that was each and every day in this town made her think of possibilities, fresh starts, renewed hope.

"Red sky at morning, sailors take warning. Red sky at night, sailor's delight," Kiley recited, remembering some snippet that she'd learned as a child. "It seems like it should be the other way around."

Tom put his right hand on her jeans-clad left leg. "Plus

there's no sailors out here, unless they like sandstorms. As for the red sky, I'd say it's because of the brush fires in the mountains."

"And that doesn't matter?"

He glanced at her curiously.

"For wherever we're going?"

"Nope."

"Can I have a hint?"

He grinned. "Nope."

"I can't believe I let a farm boy from Iowa get me out of bed at five in the morning to take me on some magical mystery tour."

Kiley shook her head in mock indignation. Since she'd had no idea where they were going and hadn't known how to dress, she'd just thrown on old jeans, a high school sweatshirt, and her Doc Martens. Fortunately, Tom was similarly dressed.

"How much further, O man of mystery?"

"Five minutes."

They continued east for one more exit, then Tom got off the freeway. On both sides of the service road were the usual chain businesses catering to interstate travelers—gas stations, Denny's, McDonald's, and the like. Suddenly, Tom turned left onto a gravel road between an Applebee's and a tire outlet. The only unusual thing was a pair of high-flying purple helium balloon clusters on either side of the lane, anchored to the ground by a stack of dirty white sandbags.

Then they were behind the stores, pulling into a huge open field that hadn't been visible from the freeway.

She whooped with delight as she saw why Tom had

brought her to this place. "Hot-air ballooning! I've always wanted to do this!"

Tom stopped the truck in a parking area that had been cordoned off with orange traffic cones. There were two dozen multicolored hot-air balloons in various states of inflation, plus hundreds of people standing around in awe as the buoyant behemoths grew to full size under the watchful eye of their handlers.

"The annual Pomona hot-air balloon race," Tom announced. "We're in it."

She threw her arms around his neck. "This is a fantastic surprise, man of mystery."

"We aim to please." He kissed her lightly. "Keep your eyes open for the Kool Threads balloon. It's red and white checked, like a tablecloth, with a KT logo on the side in black. That's our ride."

Kiley spotted the KT balloon even before she was out of the truck. "It's over to the left."

"Your airborne chariot awaits, madam. Let's go."

As they crossed the sandy field toward their balloon, Tom explained what he knew about the race. Not actually a race, it was more like a competition. One balloon would take off first, as a sort of marker for the others to follow. Then, after an hour or so of flight, the lead balloon would descend. When it was down, its crew would unfold a ten-foot-square bull's-eye. The other balloonists in the race would try to drop a fifty-pound reinforced sack of grass seed into the middle of the bull's-eye as their balloons passed high overhead. Closest to the bull's-eye won a thousand dollars.

The competing balloons came in all different shapes and sizes—golf balls and footballs, diamonds and plums. Almost all bore the logos of corporate sponsorship, which made perfect sense. Who wouldn't pay attention to a hot-air balloon soaring high overhead?

"How'd you arrange this?" Kiley asked.

"KT wants to sign me to a print-ad contract for sales in Malaysia and the Philippines, so they invited me to come for a ride. I asked them if it would be okay if I invited my girlfriend."

Tom said this last piece with special emphasis, which made Kiley feel better than she'd felt since scuba class. She realized that in his own way, he was apologizing for how he hadn't been sufficiently up-front about their relationship in the past.

"Yeah?" she asked, glancing at him.

"Definitely yeah."

A tall and cadaverously thin fellow old enough to be Kiley's grandfather, if not her great-grandfather, was standing near a wicker-basket gondola below the three-quarters-inflated KT balloon. He wore a World War II flight jacket with his black trousers, which made Kiley wonder whether he was a veteran of that conflict. He was that old.

"Howdy, howdy, welcome to Grandpa Willie's balloon." He shook Tom's hand, and then Kiley's. "I might be twice the age of them children out here, but that just means I ain't crashed yet! Been balloonin' since the fifties. Don't you worry, you're in good hands with me."

"You good?" Tom asked Kiley quietly so that Grandpa Willie wouldn't overhear.

She knew he was referring to her fear factor. "I'm good," she assured him, and prayed with all her might that she was telling the truth.

Grandpa Willie helped them both into the wicker passenger compartment. "Know why the basket's wicker? 'Cause it won't shatter if we land too hard! We just leave that part to your bones!" Grandpa Willie chortled, like it was the first time he'd ever made this lame joke.

Once they were inside the compartment, though, Grandpa Willie was all business, expertly checking the propane tanks, the burner, the bleed valve on top of the balloon, the altimeter that would tell him how high they were in the sky, and a cooler filled with ice. "And champagne," the pilot explained. "For the end of the trip. First time up for both of you?"

"Yep," Tom said, taking Kiley's hand again.

"Well then, the crew's gonna come shove us off any minute. May as well repeat after me:

"The winds will welcome me with softness
The sun will hold me in her warm hands
I will fly high and well
And God will join me in my laughter
And set me gently back down
Into the loving arms of Mother Earth."

"That's beautiful," Kiley said softly.

"Ballooner's prayer," the wizened pilot reported. "Newcomers say it at the beginning and again on landing. Unless they come to a bad end, a-course!" He cackled again at his own joke. "I'm just funnin' ya. We'll be celebrating at the end

221

with champagne." He got out a walkie-talkie from his bomber jacket, so ancient it was cracked like parched desert land, and held it to his mouth. "Flight control, this is balloon KT, Grandpa Willie at the controls, ready for ascension. This race is ours to win."

Grandpa Willie shut off the propane gas burner; the wicker passenger compartment instantly went silent. They were floating two thousand feet above Pomona, California, drifting westward at a leisurely fifteen miles an hour. The morning sun should have been baking, but the altitude made both Kiley and Tom grateful for their sweatshirts. As they looked back toward the launch area, an armada of hot-air balloons filled the sky behind them in a plethora of shapes and colors. To the west was the lead balloon, shaped like a baseball. It featured the logo of the Los Angeles Dodgers.

"Don't tell me 'cause I already know. It's better than sex," Grandpa Willie boomed. "And yes, little missy, that's more than a memory for yours truly. You kids did not invent the hoozy-whatsit-horizontal."

Kiley laughed, and so did Tom. She felt so free, so light and effervescent sailing through the sky that she didn't think she could take offense at anyone or anything.

"Now, take your ballooning." Grandpa Willie made an expansive gesture toward the sky as if he was personally responsible. "You can do it longer and there's nothing socially unacceptable about doing it by yourself."

The old man chuckled to himself as Kiley inhaled deeply, reveling in the moment. With the propane burners off and the earth a half mile below them, the feeling of riding the thermals perched in a wicker basket was exhilarating. Grandpa Willie had explained the simple physics: Cold air sank and warm air rose. When the burners were lit, filling the huge balloon with warm air, the balloon rose. When Grandpa Willie wanted to descend, he turned off the burners and bled hot air out the top of the balloon via a mechanical valve.

"I reckon it'll be another half hour before the control balloon sets down," Grandpa Willie told them. "You kids want some privacy?"

Privacy? He couldn't possibly be giving the green light to have sex up here in the sky, could he? What was he going to do, turn his back and pretend not to watch or listen? Not that Kiley was about to take the old guy up on it. She and Tom hadn't even done the "hoozy-whatsit-horizontal" yet. The first time was definitely not going to be in a hot-air balloon with an old guy four feet away.

Grandpa Willie held up a set of green headphones. "These here puppies—I put 'em on I can't hear a danged thing." He gave Tom a knowing look. "I'll be slipping 'em on now. Sometimes folks up here want some private conversating."

He put the headphones in place over his ears, turned his back, and fiddled with his propane burner.

" 'Conversating'?" Kiley echoed the old man. "I'm reasonably sure that isn't a word."

Tom chuckled. "He's quite a character."

For a long time, they gazed silently out at the world. To the far west were the office towers of downtown Los Angeles, gray apparitions in the yellowish haze of vehicle exhaust. To the east was the Mojave Desert. Up here, it didn't matter that the guy's face was lusted after by millions or that the girl was far from a supermodel. It didn't matter that she came from small-town Wisconsin or that her dreams felt bigger than the endless sky.

Tom kissed her softly. "Can you imagine your mom up here? In a hot-air balloon?"

"Never. Never ever," she corrected herself adamantly. "Panic city."

He nodded. "Yet here you are, floating in a wicker basket."

She felt so light and buoyant, so free. Her smile was luminous. "True."

"When you think about it, anything could happen," Tom went on. "The balloon could rupture. A storm could come up. A lunatic in a private plane could come through and knock us all down like a bunch of airborne bowling pins. Or, take Grandpa Willie, who appears to be old enough to have been on a first-name basis with Moses. Gramps could have a heart attack. Even Moses only lived to a hundred and twenty."

"Tom?"

"Yeah?"

"Nothing's gonna happen." Her hand went to his cheek. "That was the whole point, right?"

He gave her a rueful look. "Am I that transparent? You got me."

"Thought so."

They were passing over one of the enormous shopping centers that made people joke that the San Gabriel Valley should be renamed Twenty-nine Malls. Kiley recalled how much her mother detested malls and avoided them like the plague. Too many things could go wrong inside. Fire could break out. There could be a robbery and she'd be caught in the crossfire. There could be a power failure and a customer stampede. No, no, no.

It was enough to trigger Jeanne McCann's worst panic. Hot-air ballooning? Her mother never would have made it out of the car.

Yet here I am flying through the sky in a wicker basket with the most wonderful boy on the planet, and I'm pretty sure this is what perfect joy feels like.

"I ever mention I hate crowded elevators?" Tom asked. "I'd rather take the stairs any day of the week, and I will. My brother, Tanner? Who I met at LAX this week? Flying makes him nuts. When he and his wife went on their honeymoon, he had to take two Valium just to get through the security checkpoint, and an Ambien on the plane. Now he has this job where he has to log a hundred thousand miles a year in the air. He got a shrink who helps him get through it. He still doesn't love planes. But he can fly."

"I love the ocean," Kiley said softly.

"Yeah." He kissed her forehead. "And that's good. So if it's just going underwater that's bugging you . . . well, that we can work on."

We. He had said *we.* That, and the look in his eyes, filled her with the most wonderful confidence.

"I love my mom," she said. "So much. But . . . I guess I don't have to be her daughter in every way."

The pilot's words came back to her:

> *The winds will welcome me with softness*
> *The sun will hold me in her warm hands*
> *I will fly high and well*
> *And God will join me in my laughter*
> *And set me gently back down*
> *Into the loving arms of Mother Earth.*

225

She wrapped her arms around Tom's neck and kissed him with all the passion and love in her heart. It was a kiss, Kiley thought, worthy of flying.

"Thank you," she told him.

"You're welcome."

Kiley leaned forward and tapped Grandpa Willie on the shoulder. Startled, he turned and took off the headphones. "You two still got your clothes on?"

Kiley laughed. "Yeah, sorry to disappoint you. Is there any law about the passengers not popping the champagne until they're on the ground?"

He got a gleam in his eye and opened the cooler. Out came a bottle of Korbel—not the expensive Moët & Chandon that Platinum loved, but to Kiley it mattered not at all. "Last time I heard, California Highway Patrol is earthbound, little missy. Party on."

He handed the champagne to Tom, who opened it with a flourish and held the bottle high. "To flying high and well."

"I'll drink to that," Kiley agreed, and they did.

25

While Tom and Kiley were soaring high over the San Gabriel Valley, Esme was awakened from a deep slumber by a strange, rhythmic *thump-thump* outside her bedroom window. She scrunched deeper into her feather pillow to try to block out the sound. It was no use. *Thump-thump. Thump-thump. Thump-thump.*

Shit. She opened her eyes, turned onto her back, and listened. *Thump-thump. Thump-thump.* What the hell was that?

She pulled on an old pair of gym shorts and an even older navy blue T-shirt, and padded barefoot through the guesthouse. She was relieved to see that Tarshea's door was closed tightly. It meant she was still asleep, and not at the house whipping up breakfast for the girls, the staff, and probably the Dodgers, too. For once, Esme could do her job. Maybe it would restore some of Diane's faith in her.

As the erratic noise outside the guesthouse continued

unabated, she followed the sound outside. It was Jonathan, shirtless in cutoff jeans and Chuck Taylors. As she watched unnoticed, he picked up the dribble of the basketball in his hands and spun to his left, narrating his own play-by-play loudly enough for Esme to hear every word.

"Lakers down by two, two seconds left! Kobe with the ball, looking to get free! Still guarded by Ginobili! Kobe at the three-point line whirls and fires!"

With that, Jonathan spun and took a jump shot over his invisible opponent. Esme watched the ball arc high and then clang off the rim. His tanned, taut torso gleamed with a thin veil of sweat. Damn, he looked good.

"And the Lakers lose again!"

Usually Esme was charmed by Jonathan's boyish enthusiasm for sports. Not today. There were too many unanswered questions.

"You gotta make that shot," she advised.

The ball had rebounded out to the left and rolled to a stop against one of the orange trees. As he retrieved it, he shrugged. "It's hard, with Manu guarding me."

"Well, do it quietly. Tarshea is still asleep." Esme cocked her chin toward the guesthouse.

"Nope." Jonathan dribbled the ball toward her. "Diane took her and the twins to LAX for her final interview. Something about how Ann Marie wanted to observe Tarshea with the children."

Esme slid onto the wooden bench under the fragrant jasmine bush just outside the front door. "The airport? That doesn't make any sense."

Jonathan hooked one last shot. "She's flying to San Francisco for the morning for a meeting with Levi Strauss. This was her only free time slot." He sat next to Esme and casually slung an arm around her. "It's good to see you. This movie is gonna kick my ass."

She eyed him coolly. "Unless I kick it first."

He swiped a forearm across his sweaty forehead. "You're pissed that I didn't call you back right away? Is that it?"

"Partly."

He shook his head humbly. "You haven't spent enough time on a movie set. There's no privacy. Sometimes there's no cell coverage."

"Do I look like I got stupid all of a sudden?" Esme queried. "You had a lot of options and we both know it."

"What, you think I was deliberately dissing you?"

"Were you?"

He draped an arm across the back of the bench and touched her shoulder lightly. "This director, Laszlo—the guy is deeply strange. Like for example, he collects all the cell phones on the set."

"Oh please. Beverly Baylor would never give up her phone. Or Mischa?"

"Oh yeah they would," Jonathan said. "And did. The guy's a genius and everyone knows it. You want to work with a genius, you put up with insanity."

Esme was still skeptical. "Maybe."

"Definitely," Jonathan insisted. "We all did. That is, until he got fired last night."

"What? How does a director get fired?"

Esme's father had recently hung a hummingbird feeder just outside the entrance to the guesthouse and filled it with reddened sugar water to attract the maximum number of birds. Before Jonathan could answer Esme's question, a pair of ruby-throated beauties buzzed down from the sky and hovered at the feeder, taking turns sucking the nectar with their long beaks and tongues.

He gestured toward the tiny, whirring birds. "See how they're cooperating? Laszlo is the opposite. I mean, yeah, sure the guy has a rep. But this time he went too far. Like rewriting the script without telling Sara—she's the executive producer—"

"The nice one. I met her," Esme reminded him.

"Yeah, so anyway, she blew a gasket and dumped him last night. I think Bobby Roth is coming in to replace him. We're way behind our shooting schedule, improvising shit to try to cut pages. It's just been totally insane."

Esme was still dubious about Jonathan's too-busy-to-make-a-phone-call thing, but she moved on anyway. "You know I did Beverly's tattoo the other night?"

"Yup. She's been showing everyone on the set. Gotta wonder about a woman in her forties who tattoos a cowboy on her inner thigh, huh?" His hand found the back of her neck and caressed it gently. "You did an amazing job, though. I hope you charged her a mint. She gave your number to lots of people."

Esme hesitated. Jonathan was acting as if nothing was wrong, as if he had nothing to hide.

Well, she'd see about that.

"Beverly told me that Mackenzie is working wardrobe. I wanted to know if you got her the job."

"*That's* what this is about?"

230

She swatted his arm. "Wipe that stupid smile off your face!"

"Oh my God, Esme. You've got to be kidding." He started to laugh. "Who do you think I am? My father on one of his shows? My stepmother with one of her charity parties? That I can tell people on a movie production team to jump and they'll ask how high? God, Esme. I got hired two days before they started shooting. I don't have that kind of power!"

Esme felt blood rush to her face. "You had nothing to do with it."

"Esme. If I had wanted Mackenzie to be a wardrobe assistant, do you think I would have invited you to the set?"

"Guys have been known to do such things, Jonathan." She shook her long dark hair off her face. "Who hired her, then?"

"The line producer hires the wardrobe chick, and the wardrobe chick—that would be Helen Walley—hires her crew. Mackenzie has worked for her before. Jesus, Esme. I hardly ever even see her, she's in the goddamn trailer all day."

"But Beverly said that Mackenzie said that—"

Inside the guesthouse, the phone rang. Esme rose and hurried to her door. "I've got to get this, it might be about the kids."

"Mackenzie said what?" Jonathan called.

That you two were still together.

"Esme Castaneda, Goldhagen residence." Ignoring Jonathan's query, she answered the phone.

"Esme, it's Ann Marie, calling from my jet. Have Tarshea and Diane returned?"

"Not yet," Esme reported.

"When they do please have Tarshea call my cell after ten o'clock. I'll be available then. And no need to hold back good news. Tell her the job is hers. She can start tomorrow morning."

"Oh, that's great!" Esme exclaimed.

She got Ann Marie's number, assured her that Tarshea would call immediately, and danced back out the door to Jonathan. "Tarshea just got a nanny job!"

She plopped down in his lap, happy for Tarshea and thrilled for herself. Once Tarshea moved out, they could still be friends. Maybe even good friends.

"Excellent." Jonathan kissed her lightly. He wrapped his arms around her and held her against his bare chest. "Does this mean you forgive me?"

"No," Esme said, but she kissed him again as she said it. "Next time text me, or something."

"Tough girl," he teased, one hand slipping under her T-shirt to caress her back.

She twisted around and gave him a smoldering kiss in return. Just as she was getting thoroughly lost in the moment, he pushed her away.

"Wha—?"

Then she saw what he did: Tarshea was running down the redbrick path from the main house with the twins in tow, and Diane was bringing up the rear.

Shit. Diane's rules expressly forbade Esme from being alone with Jonathan on the Goldhagen property.

"Did she see us?" she whispered.

"Doubtful," Jonathan replied. He grabbed the basketball

and held it over his lap to cover his anatomical reaction to Esme's kiss. She stifled a laugh.

As usual, when the twins saw their older brother, they screamed with joy and dashed into his arms. They adored Jonathan, and as yet had none of the too-cool-to-show-it of so many other Hollywood kids even their young age.

"*Yon-o-tin!*" Easton squealed, hugging him tight. "Can we see *película*?"

"That means—" Esme began.

"Movie," Tarshea filled in as Diane joined them. Esme noticed her employer beaming at the Jamaican girl. Then Diane looked from Esme to Jonathan and back to Esme again, clearly unhappy to see them alone in the same location.

"Jonathan," she said curtly, nodding at her stepson.

"I just stopped by to say hello," Jonathan explained.

"I'm sure," Diane said dryly.

Tarshea knelt down to the twins. "We can't see Jonathan's movie yet," she told them. "*No está lista todavía.*"

"Exactly. I guess." Jonathan scooped up the girls, much to their squealing delight, one under each arm. "How about I make you big ice cream sundaes for breakfast?"

"Yay!" the girls cheered.

"Not too big, Jonathan," Diane cautioned.

"Oh, definitely not," Jonathan agreed, but winked at the twins. When he carried the girls past their mother and on up toward the main house, it left Esme alone with Tarshea and Diane.

"We've got news," Diane announced.

Okay, that was good. If Diane was going to say anything

about finding Esme and Jonathan together, she wasn't going to do it now.

"Great news. Really great," Tarshea added, grinning at Diane.

"I think I'm up to speed," Esme responded. "Ann Marie called. It really is great. Congratulations. I hope you love working for her."

Tarshea looked puzzled. "She offered me the job? When?"

"Just a few minutes ago. She called. I figured she called you on your cell."

Tarshea shook her head.

"Well, it's nice to be wanted." Diane looped her arm around Tarshea's narrow waist. "Not that it will make any difference. Right?"

What were they talking about?

"No problem," Tarshea assured Diane.

"Well, that's a relief," Diane said. "Tarshea, you'll just have to telephone Ann Marie and tell her that you appreciate her generous offer but are graciously declining. I'll get her involved in FAB next summer, there will be no hard feelings."

"Yes, ma'am, I'll do that," Tarshea agreed.

Esme held up her hand. "Um, excuse me. You're turning down the job you wanted?"

"You didn't talk to her, Tarshea?" Diane was surprised.

"Not until I was certain, ma'am."

"Well then!" Her boss spread her arms wide. "I felt it was only fair to let Tarshea do this interview and make her own decision. I've offered her a job, and she's accepted. We're going to be a two-nanny family. You don't mind sharing your guesthouse, do you, Esme?"

"Oh, no," Esme said, careful to keep her voice neutral. "Not at all."

"So this works out really well," Diane concluded. "It'll be perfect when you start school, Esme. Tarshea can stay with the children during the day, and you can take them in the evenings and on weekends. Fall is charity event season, so I'll be extremely busy."

Esme was in a state of mild shock. Yes, there were plenty of families at the country club with two nannies. They alternated shifts, or one worked during the week and the other did nights and weekends. Occasionally, she'd heard of the whole entourage—parents, kids, and double nannies—jetting off for a vacation together.

Tarshea gave Esme a warm hug. "It's going to be great. You are the best friend I could ever have."

"Well then, that's settled. I've got my masseuse coming in a half hour. I'm going to go up to the main house and shower. Oh, could one of you make sure Cleo gets to the groomer this afternoon? Their mobile unit is on the fritz. I want her bow aqua this month and her nails painted aqua with little white flowers."

"No problem, ma'am," Tarshea said. She pulled a small notebook out of her purse and jotted down a few notes.

"Oh sweetie, I'll get you a Palm Pilot. You two girls sit down and work out a schedule for the next two weeks," Diane continued. "I want the twins covered from seven in the morning to nine at night, seven days a week. Of course there will be times when neither of you will be needed, and sometimes both of you. I'll give a day's warning, how'll that be?"

"No problem, ma'am," Tarshea said again.

"Tarshea?" Diane raised her eyebrows.

"Yes, ma'am?"

"You're going to have to start calling me Diane. After all, now . . . this is home." She turned and headed up the path for the main house.

"You are okay with this, Esme? You helped me so much." Tarshea's eyes oozed gratitude.

"I thought you wanted your own job, your own place to live."

"I love the twins and I love you, Esme. You've been good to me. You are a good person. I even wear your clothes and you didn't say anything because you know I am just a poor Jamaican girl tryin' to make my way here in America. You think I didn't notice that? 'Nuff respect, Esme. 'Nuff respect."

Esme sighed. There was really no choice but to make the best of it. Unless she wanted to quit and do tattoos, that is. "Let's go plan our schedule, then." She headed into the guesthouse, with Tarshea right behind her.

"Jonathan Goldhagen is mighty tighty whitey, you know," Tarshea mused.

Esme flopped onto the living room couch. "Which means?"

"One fine white boy." Tarshea sat in the wing chair and took out her notebook again. "That's what the girls who work at the resorts in Jamaica say about the cute white male tourists. Are you in love with him?"

"Why do you ask?"

Tarshea shrugged. "Just wondered. The white American boys, when they come to Jamaica, they think the Jamaican girls are very exotic." Then she laughed. "Maybe he think that about you."

"Did you hook up with some white American guy in Jamaica?" Esme asked.

"Me? Oh, no. I am still a good church-girl, as my mudda would say." Tarshea nibbled on the end of her pen. "I'm not in Jamaica anymore, though. So this is why I asked if you love the boy."

"Because if I don't love him you'll move in on him?" Esme asked sharply.

Tarshea gave Esme a wide-eyed look. "But you do love him, sister. So no problem."

They went on to create a schedule for the next week, but Esme couldn't get Tarshea's words out of her mind. Somehow, when Tarshea said "no problem," the feeling Esme got was just the opposite.

26

"Where are we going again?" Martina was so excited that she was bouncing against the seat belt in the back of Kat's black BMW 323i.

"Easy, sweet pea," Lydia cautioned. "It's my first time driving this car."

Before they'd departed the estate, Kat had given Lydia a lecture. The 323i, originally manufactured in 1978, had been lovingly restored to pristine condition by a former BMW engineer now living in San Diego. There were no more being made. Translation: Be careful. No dents.

"Remember, you just got your learner's permit," Aunt Kat had admonished before turning over the car keys.

"X will be with me," Lydia had assured her aunt.

X was the moms' driver. Seriously skinny, with short spiky blond hair and cheekbones that would make a model envious, he and Lydia had become great friends. In fact, he'd escorted

Lydia on her first major shopping spree when she'd arrived in Los Angeles, a sort of "Queer Eye for the Straight Girl" outing to Rodeo Drive. Though X was one hundred percent gay, Billy had been his best friend since their childhood together in Redondo Beach.

X was smart, funny, and very much in the Hollywood-know. His friendship meant a lot to Lydia. She shuddered to think what it would do to that friendship if and when he found out how she'd betrayed Billy. He surely would find out, too. Why wouldn't Billy mention it to him? They were the kind of guy friends who really talked to each other.

Ugh. How *did* everything get so complicated?

The look on Billy's face last night with Luis. She'd expected Billy to rush down the hallway and punch his lights out. She would have been happy to do it herself. He didn't. Instead, he'd just closed the door and quietly asked, "Is that true?"

When the moment called for it, Lydia could be a brilliant liar. If ever a moment had called for an artful fabrication, this was it. And she had it, almost: Luis was in love with her. He was making up this story because she'd rejected him. Yes, he'd brought her the huge dinner invitation, but she'd done the smart thing by ignoring it.

Yet there was hard physical evidence: her own T-shirt in her hands. Worse than that was the guilt she felt radiate from her face.

"I can explain," she began.

"Don't try. Just go into the bathroom. When you come out, I won't be here."

She tried to protest, but it was hopeless. Five minutes later, he was gone.

"Serious oral fixation."

X's voice pulled her out of her depressed recollections, as the southbound traffic on La Cienega Boulevard inched along. Though it was midmorning, they were stuck in bumper-to-bumper congestion. "I'd cut off my right hand for a stick of gum right now."

"I have some!" Martina cried from the backseat, delving into the depths of her new Hello Kitty purse. "I guess chewing gum helps you not to smoke, huh, X?"

X winced. "Busted. How did you know I smoke?"

"Oh, I know a lot more than people give me credit for." Martina handed over a slightly bent foil-wrapped stick of gum and leaned back contentedly on the white leather rear seat. "This is so fun, just the three of us."

Since Anya and Kat had taken Jimmy to the golf course to play his very first round—Lydia hoped he would hook one right into Luis's teeth—Martina had been put in Lydia's charge for the day. She was supposed to take her to an orientation meeting at the United States Soccer Federation facility in Carson for some junior camp that Anya wanted her to attend, not that Martina had ever expressed the least interest in the game.

Martina had moaned so much about the soccer thing that Lydia decided to make the excursion more interesting by giving Martina some new targets for blow dart practice. After a quick consultation with X, who promised to keep their outing a secret, they decided the area around the old oil rigs near the airport would be perfect. Though the wells were still functioning, few went into those hills but the occasional oil roughneck. It would be perfect for long-range shooting.

They all dressed in shorts, T-shirts, and running shoes, since X told her those hills were one of the hottest places in all of L.A. Even Martina had agreed to wear shorts, albeit baggy ones, and a long-sleeved T-shirt, albeit baggier.

"You know, Lydia, Momma Kat doesn't let anyone drive this car," Martina sang out from the backseat. "She must really trust you. Where are we going?"

Lydia didn't know whether to laugh or cry. She felt like the least trustworthy person on the planet. In fact, she felt about as trustworthy as Anya.

Again she wondered: How did everything get so complicated?

Though she didn't long for Amazonia, this sort of crap never happened in the jungle. The Amas had a much different view of sexual activity than did twenty-first-century Americans. If a guy wanted to have sex, he did. If a woman wanted to have sex, she did. It was just sex. Yet Lydia knew that if Billy had done to her what she'd done to him, she'd be madder than hell, just as she expected Susan and Kat would be when they learned about the colonel and Anya the Evil. Maybe she should just drive to Billy's place and camp out until he showed up. No, that reeked way too much of what loathsome Luis had just done. Something more creative, then. There had to be a way.

"Plant hopping, dear one?" X asked, peering at her. "I've never heard Lydia Chandler this quiet."

"Fine . . . Just concentrating on the road."

"Nonsense. I can tell when your wheels are turning. From the look on your face, I'm seeing overdrive."

For the briefest moment, Lydia contemplated confiding in

X. Maybe he'd understand. Maybe he would even be support-ive. Most important, since he knew Billy so well, maybe he could help her come up with the plan to win him back.

She glanced in the rearview mirror. Oh no. While she was thinking and driving, Martina had not only opened the box that contained her blowgun, but also had actually assem-bled the components. "Hold on. What in tarnation do you think you're doing with that? You know the rules!"

"Well, you were ignoring me," Martina retorted defiantly. "You broke the rules first."

X twisted around to regard the primitive weapon. "How phallic."

"What's 'phallic'?" Martina asked.

"It was a kind of Roman column," X improvised. "That tube reminds me of it."

That was so quick and funny that in spite of her current ru-minations, Lydia laughed aloud.

"You didn't even say what a good job I did putting the blowgun together all by myself," Martina groused.

"Don't load it until we get there," Lydia said.

"Can't you just tell me how much further?"

Lydia looked at X for guidance; she'd never been in this part of L.A. before.

He looked out the window to catch the intersection. "Fif-teen minutes or so. Maybe twenty-five if the traffic doesn't get any better."

The traffic stayed brutal. They'd passed the intersection with Venice Boulevard five minutes before and were just com-ing up on the traffic light at National when X instructed Lydia to turn west, thinking that maybe they could outflank this unholy mess. She edged into the right lane and halted briefly at the red light before she made the right-on-red turn onto National.

Just as she did, a bright blue Spyder cut her off so badly that she was blocked nearly against the curb.

"Jackass!" she bellowed.

"Ix-nay the anguage-lay," X warned, cocking his chin toward the backseat and Martina.

"Well, he is a jackass."

"I speak pig latin, you know," Martina said with self-importance.

Instead of backing away from his foolish mistake, the driver of the Spyder rolled down the passenger-side window. Great. She had plenty to say to him. Or her. Then Lydia saw who the driver was, and nearly slammed her foot on the gas of the Beemer to shove the Spyder into Orange County with the driver in it.

She rolled down her own window. "Get your fucking car out of the way! And stop fucking following me!"

Luis grinned. *¡Hola, mamacita!*

"You know this guy?" X was incredulous, but Lydia ignored him.

"Move your car, Luis! Or I will make your life a thing of misery!"

"How's your ex-boyfriend?" Luis jeered. "Want Luis to kiss it and make it all better?"

The light changed to green; people in the vehicles stacked up behind them started to honk. But there was nothing Lydia could do. Except . . .

"Excuse me. I have to go kill that guy."

Lydia started to open the door, but X yanked her arm. "I don't know what went down with Billy, but are you insane? You're in the middle of a traffic jam in a quarter-million-dollar car with a fifth-grade girl in the backseat! Get ahold of yourself. You want to be a statistic?"

"Hey, I recognize him, he's Jimmy's golf teacher!" Martina cried. "Is he your enemy, Lydia?"

"He's a loathsome pot of piss, is what he is."

"Slide over and let me take the wheel," X advised. "I'll get us out of here."

"I wouldn't give him the satisfaction."

Lydia rammed the gearshift into reverse as the vehicles behind her pulled into the center lane to get around the Beemer. The passing drivers honked angrily; several offered Lydia their upraised middle fingers. But at least their departure gave her a little room. That's what she thought, anyway, until Luis edged his Spyder even closer to the BMW, and she was trapped again.

"You think I'm gonna let you just get away with that shit? I'm not letting you leave, Lydia. I'll follow you!"

"The man is a maniac!" X yanked out his BlackBerry to call 911, then Martina's voice stopped him.

"Leave us alone!"

Lydia whirled around. Her cousin's window was down; she had the blowgun up to her lips, the plastic tubing reaching far outside the car.

"Martina, don't even—"

Too late.

The dart struck its target dead-on. It struck directly into his right front tire, which was deflating before their eyes with a high-pitched whistle.

"Try to follow us now, you asshole!" Martina yelled out the window. "Come on, Lydia, go!"

Lydia managed to back away, and Luis tried to follow, but it was impossible with his flat. As she turned onto National and then sped away, she saw him in the rearview mirror pounding his fist on the hood of his disabled vehicle.

"You shouldn't have done that, Martina. Remember how I told you that the blowgun wasn't a toy?"

"He was your enemy," Martina explained.

"Rules are still rules, sweet pea. However . . ." She caught her cousin's gaze in the rearview mirror. "That was a hell of a shot."

"Thanks."

Martina sat up a little straighter, shoulders back, hair off her face, and beamed.

Lydia couldn't help herself. Life may have gotten complicated, but she was still damn proud.

27

"Whee! More, Esme, more!"

"Okay. Hold on, both of you!"

Timing her push perfectly, Esme was able to put her right hand in the small of Weston's back and her left hand in the small of Easton's. With some gentle pressure, she helped the laws of physics, and both girls swung skyward on the magnificent custom-designed teak playground-style swing set that now occupied the grass near the tennis court. With three swings, a slide, a tree house, a whirly-round, and a jungle gym, it was as elaborate as the one at the country club, only on a smaller scale.

"Whee!" Easton pumped her legs, trying to go higher. "Fun!"

It was midafternoon of the same day. Esme was alone with the kids, since Diane had brought Tarshea to Fred Segal's clothing store. If Tarshea was going to be working for her, she needed a presentable wardrobe. Esme didn't mind, really, since Tarshea would take over for her at five. That was good, since Lydia had summoned her and Kiley to dinner at Taste, the Italian place on Melrose Avenue.

"One day, you will be a wonderful mother, Esme."

She heard the voice behind her—the voice she'd recognize anywhere. It was her own wonderful mother, Estella Castaneda. When she turned and waved, she saw that her mom was dressed in the black maid's uniform that the Goldhagens required. Though they worked for the Goldhagens too, Esme's parents rarely crossed paths with her during the day. This was a treat.

Especially, she thought, *because I have a treat for her.*

"Mama!" she exclaimed, embracing her warmly. "It's so good to see you."

"It's a quiet day up at the house. I thought I would see how you were with the girls."

Esme gave the twins each another push. "Can you stay for a minute?"

Her mother nodded, so Esme stopped the swings and suggested that the girls have a contest to see who could be the first to go up and down the slide twenty times. After they hugged Mrs. Castaneda, they miraculously agreed, as long as Esme would count them off. An *uno-dos-tres* later, they were clambering over each other, laughing as they tussled to see who would be the first to get to the top of the slide.

"Like I said," Estella observed. She and Esme stood side by side, watching the girls play. "You will be a wonderful mother. No rush, though."

Esme dug into the pocket of her jeans. "Speaking of wonderful. I have something for *my* wonderful mother."

"What could you possibly have for me?"

"Just this." She pressed a wad of bills into her mother's right hand. They were all hundreds. Eleven of them.

"Esme? What is this?" Estella stared at her open hand. "Where did you get this? Tell me that Junior's boys didn't—"

"Oh no, it's completely legal. I just did some tattoos for some friends of Jonathan. That's all. They paid me well."

"How much did they pay you?"

Esme explained how she'd made more money in one night of tattooing than in one week at the Goldhagens'.

Estella's eyes narrowed. "So much money for a tattoo? I can't believe it."

"Neither can I. And other friends are calling me now."

Señora Castaneda looked closely at her daughter. "You are a smart girl. Do not do a dumb thing."

"How can making money be dumb, Mama? I'll give it to you and Papa. You've given me so much."

"I heard about how Diane hired that girl from Jamaica as another nanny. She will live with you, too. You are thinking maybe you should quit this place, go back to the Echo, and do tattoos full-time. ¿Verdad?"

Esme didn't lie to her mother. "Verdad. Yes. I thought that."

Now her mother smiled. "Good. That shows you are smart. You will show you are smarter by staying at this job and going to that good high school. Your father has no education. I have no education. Our daughter will have education. What happens if one day you wake up and your hands do not work, like your Tía Consuela up in Fresno? What would you do then?"

Consuela was Esme's favorite aunt. A seamstress for many

years, she'd been stricken by arthritis at the age of thirty-five, and was now on disability.

"That won't happen to me," Esme said as she watched Weston go feet-first down the slide.

"That is what your aunt told me, too. I am not saying no tattoos. Do them. Save the money for college. If you do not trust yourself to save it, give it to me and Papa and we will save it for you."

"But you have so little!" Esme protested. "I really wanted you to spend what I give you on yourselves."

Estella shook her head sadly. "Maybe when you are a mother, you will understand, *hija mía*. Watching you save money for college *is* spending it on ourselves."

She unfolded the hundred-dollar bills in her hand, smoothed them out, and then gave them back to Esme. "You know what to do with this?"

"In the bank, Mama. In the bank."

"Exactly." Estella hugged her daughter tight. "That is why you are such a smart girl. And why Papa and I are so very proud of you."

28

"Now that Kiley has arrived, let me announce that I have convened this meeting of the nanny brigade for a very special reason," Lydia intoned gravely.

Just like Esme, Kiley had been summoned to Taste, the überhip restaurant just east of La Cienega on Melrose. She found her friends nursing iced cappuccinos at one of the square wooden tables on the small outdoor patio that faced the street. Though it was only six o'clock, the patio was already crowded with an eclectic mix of chic Eurotrash, grungy musician types, and talent agents in their designer suits meeting clients for dinner.

"Which is?" Esme asked. She dipped a forefinger into the cinnamon-scented whipped cream that topped her drink and touched it to her tongue. "By the way, Kiley, we ordered. Pizzettas, which are small pizzas. Good?"

"Good. So why the emergency meal? I had to promise the colonel overtime tonight."

"Simple," Lydia explained. "At approximately ten p.m. Pacific time last night, my life sunk to the sixth rung of hell."

Kiley raised her eyebrows. "And yet under this horrific duress you still managed to put on three coats of mascara, lip gloss, and perhaps the shortest skirt I've ever seen." There was a basket of homemade bread on the table, and she took one of the crusty rolls. It was absolutely delicious, redolent of butter and spices she couldn't place.

Lydia smoothed the tiny Stella McCartney flounce of citron silk she'd worn with Jimmy Choo silver-feathered sandals. "Lydia's first law of life: When you feel your worst, it is important to look your best," she decreed as a buff guy in sweatpants and a muscle shirt jogged by on Melrose. He stopped, flashed an appreciative smile over his shoulder, then continued on his way.

Oh my God. When Kiley was out with Lydia, it was Lydia who got the looks. Or sultry Esme, who was wearing tight black Bebe capris and an even tighter black sleeveless T-shirt. But unless Kiley's eyes were playing tricks, the hot jogger had looked right at her.

Esme's brow knit together. "Do you know him?"

"Never saw him before in my life," Kiley admitted.

Huh. She was wearing a white embroidered off-the-shoulder peasant blouse that Platinum had bestowed upon her, along with tan jeans. Her hair was freshly washed, and for once she was wearing it down; it fell in graceful burnished waves over her shoulders. Around her neck was a silver chain from which dangled two charms—a silver porpoise and a gold hot-air balloon. She wrapped her fingers around the charms and grinned without realizing it.

"New jewelry?" Esme asked as their waiter—an Italian guy with the build of a soccer player and curly black hair—put some extra pizza toppings on their table: small plates of diced garlic, fresh grated parmesan cheese, and minced red onion.

"Yep. From Tom."

Lydia narrowed her eyes at Kiley. "That's why you look so happy. It went well last night."

"More than that." Kiley quickly relayed the story of the balloon ride and how good she'd felt up there. "When we came down to earth, he gave me this necklace."

"Subtle symbolism," Lydia cracked.

"Nope. Good guy," Esme said softly. "Food's on me, Kiley, by the way. I'm flush."

"Yeah," Lydia chimed in. "Esme's now a tattoo entrepreneur. Hey . . . maybe we should start a tattoo business."

"No!" Kiley and Esme declared simultaneously.

"Hey, how come you didn't bring Tarshea with you?" Kiley asked Esme. She took another of the spiced rolls, worried for a moment about the carb and calorie count, and then bit into it anyway.

"She's working."

"She got the gig with Ann Marie?"

Esme nodded darkly. "Oh, she got it all right. But she didn't take it. Why? Diane made her a better offer. Guys, I now have a co-nanny."

The Italian waiter brought two pizzettas and placed them on the riser-stand. Only eight inches across, one was covered in cremini mushrooms, goat cheese, mozzarella, and slow-roasted tomatoes. The other featured an array of mouth-watering vegetables and parmesan cheese. Both smelled delicious. "Enjoy, ladies. The others will come soon. Can I bring anything else?"

"Two other friends who look like you?" Lydia joked.

"Ah, *bella*." The waiter bowed. "You ask for the specialty of the house. I go and talk to the chef. Enjoy."

He moved off; Kiley was the first to bite into a slice. It was superb. "Is it good to have help, Esme?"

"I sound like a small-minded bitch if I say no."

"Some of my favorite people are small-minded bitches," Lydia said. "She's great with the twins but she's sharing your house and she's cramping your style. You don't want her around. Am I right?"

"More than," Esme agreed. "I keep thinking . . . Well, if I can make a mint doing tattoos for all these rich Hollywood types, why be a nanny? But my mother told me to stay. So I'm staying."

"If you quit, you'd have to go back to the Echo," Kiley said.

"It's funny, really. When I first moved in, I couldn't stand the quiet. Now I love living someplace beautiful and serene, and so, so much more than I could ever afford." Esme slumped back in her chair. "I'm not proud of that."

Kiley downed the last of her cappuccino and edged her chair closer to the table as a pair of writer types—jeans, T-shirts, baseball caps, unshaven, glasses—sat down at the table behind her. "Don't be so hard on yourself."

"Damn right," Lydia said. "Keep your job, keep doing tattoos, and run to the bank."

"At least I can help out my parents. I tried to give my mom most of what I made. She wouldn't take it. So I slipped two hundred bucks into her pocketbook this afternoon. I don't think she's found it yet." Esme took a thoughtful bite of pizza.

Lydia put up a "hold on" hand. "Y'all, I hate to interrupt this joyfest, but while your lives are all peachy keen and everything, I believe I called this meeting to bring attention to the shithole I'm in. The least you could do is act curious."

"It's just that you never get depressed, Lydia," Kiley said. "You always handle everything."

"You think? How about this tidbit: I found out who Anya is doing. Guess who?"

"Ellen? Rosie? Anne Heche?" Esme guessed.

"Anne Heche isn't gay anymore, at least that's what she says," Lydia corrected. "Anyway, none of them."

"Some lipstick lesbian from the tennis circuit?" Kiley ventured.

"Nope. In fact, there will be no lipstick left on the Merry Matron of Moscow's collar. She's gone Heche. Way, way Heche." She grinned mischievously. "Does 'McCann! Shape up or ship out!' ring a bell?"

No flipping way. The colonel?

"Anya and the colonel? I thought all they played was golf and chess. How'd you find out?"

"Kiley dear. I saw them at the country club with his hand on her ass."

"When? Why didn't you call me?"

"I did call you. Last night. You were in too big a hurry to hook up with Model Man."

"How about Kat? Does she know?"

Lydia shook her head. "Still have to tell her. I'm dreading it."

"Anya and the colonel . . . That's sick."

Esme put down a half-eaten slice of pizza. "People cheat all the time, Kiley. I keep expecting to catch Jonathan with his ex."

"But if you're in a relationship, you have to have trust."

"Get over yourself, Kiley." Esme scoffed. "You were wigging out about Tom because you thought he was with Marym or some other hot model. You weren't exactly so full of trust."

Esme was right, and Kiley knew it. Maybe it was always true that someone had more power in any relationship, and the person who had less power would always feel a little insecure, a little frayed around the edges. For her, it was that Tom was objectively a much better-looking guy than she was a girl. For Esme, it was that she was poor and Latina, involved with a rich white guy. For Lydia . . . She had no idea.

"Okay," Kiley acknowledged. "Esme has a point. But how is your life a—?"

"Billy isn't speaking to me."

"What?" Kiley dabbed at a spot of tomato sauce she felt on her chin. "Why would he do that?"

"It's Luis's fault. First, he started following me. Then he started stalking me. Then he showed up at this hotel where Billy and I were spending the night and brought a little gift. The T-shirt I left at his house a few weeks ago. What a mess."

"You're in trouble," Esme said.

"No kidding." Lydia pushed her plate away. "In my entire seventeen years on this planet, this is the first time I have ever hated myself."

Kiley felt bad for her. This was not the time to point out yet again how stupid the whole drunk-sex-with-a-near-stranger incident had been. Nor did she want to rub salt in a very open wound by reminding Lydia that she'd advised her to simply 'fess up to Billy in the first place.

"I *know* there is a way out," Lydia said. "I just have to figure out the right angle."

"How about honesty?" Kiley cut herself another slice of pizza.

Lydia gave Kiley a baleful look. "Highly overrated. You know that old saying, 'The truth shall set you free'? Well, it would set me free, all right. Free from him. Forever." She folded her arms. "Nope. The truth thing is so not an option here."

Esme rubbed her forehead. "Well then, *chica*. You need one hell of a kick-ass cover story. Something like . . . you were . . . at Luis's house because he was loaning you his car. He has a cat. You held his cat. The cat barfed on your shirt. Luis offered to wash it. Then he started acting like an asshole, so you didn't even want it—"

"Back!" Lydia finished for her. "Which means Luis lied to Billy and said he had sex with me because I bruised his manly Latin ego! Esme, that's *brilliant*."

"Hold on, you guys," Kiley said. "Lies and then more lies . . . How can that end any way except badly?"

"Well, honey. I don't have Billy right now. So I'd say it's already ending badly," Lydia said.

"Let's deal with the Anya thing first," Esme advised, practical as usual. "You need to find a way to talk to your aunt. But I think Kiley should keep her mouth shut."

Kiley put a hand to her forehead. She felt as if she was in a completely different universe from the one in which her friends were operating. "Wait. I like Susan. Now that I know, how can I not tell her?"

"Easy," Lydia answered. "You didn't see Anya and the colonel yourself. You'd just be gossiping."

"I don't know if that's fair." Kiley pursed her lips.

"I don't think the world is fair," Esme said, her voice gentle. "In fact, I know it isn't. But that's Kat's decision to make. Not yours."

"But what about loyalty. What about love?"

Esme opened her hands face-up. "People make mistakes, Kiley. Kat and Anya, the colonel and Susan—let them work that out on their own. Okay?"

Kiley nodded.

"As for Billy," Esme went on, "Lydia knows she screwed things up. But Luis screwed things up even worse. Why should she lose Billy forever over it?"

Why, indeed? Kiley really didn't have an answer. Except that maybe both of her friends were dead wrong.

"If Billy really, truly cares about you, Lydia, maybe he'd understand."

"Oh, please," Esme scoffed. "You are like the last of the innocents. Say Tom has drunken sex with some hot model. He tells you about it afterward and says oops, sorry. What would you do?"

"Cry," Kiley admitted.

"And you'd never trust him again," Lydia added. "Not that I'm judging you."

The Italian waiter appeared again. "Sorry. The chef was very busy. No other waiters are in the oven. Anything else?" He looked at the half-eaten pizzettas on the table. "I can wrap those to go."

"That would be great," Esme told him. "And I'll take the check."

"I'll be right back." The waiter headed back inside.

"So, what are you going to do?" Kiley asked Lydia when he was out of earshot.

Lydia pushed her choppy bangs out of her eyes. "Okay, ladies, here's the game plan." She held up a forefinger. "One: About Anya and the colonel? I'll bite the bullet and tell my aunt what I saw. But Kiley, I am asking you: Don't say a word. Okay?" She gave Kiley a questioning look.

Kiley hesitated. Could she keep her mouth shut, at least for the time being? It was true that she had no evidence herself. But if she ever saw something between Anya and the colonel with her own two eyes—well, that would be completely different. Finally, she nodded.

"And two," Lydia counted off. "I use Esme's brilliant cover story with Billy."

"How does that work? He won't talk to you," Kiley reminded her.

"I'll work on X. X will get to Billy. But you two have to help me."

"How?"

"Call Billy and back me up."

Kiley balked. "I don't know, Lydia."

"Kiley. You know I'd do it for you."

This was true. She thought about the time Lydia was there for Esme when some gang members were threatening her.

When it came to supporting her friends, Lydia's loyalty knew no limits. Could Kiley be less loyal?

To Kiley's shock and amazement, there were tears in Lydia's eyes. "I'm not claiming to be a saint. But what pisses me off above everything else is this disgusting, weak, and mealy-mouthed truth: I'm in love with Billy, and an asshole of a guy went and ruined it. So I'm asking y'all—both of you. Don't let a stupid mistake and a stupider asshole ruin everything. Help me get Billy back."

Esme nodded firmly. "Of course."

As her friends looked at her expectantly, Kiley knew in her heart that on some moral level, this was wrong. But maybe the kind of friendship she had with Esme and Lydia was a bigger right than the wrong of backing up Lydia's lie.

"Okay," she told them. "I'm in."

About the Author

Raised in Bel Air, Melody Mayer is the oldest daughter of a fourth-generation Hollywood family and has outlasted countless nannies.